THE
APOCALYPSE
OF

CALEB T. BRABHAM

CREATION HOUSE
A STRANG COMPANY

THE APOCALYPSE OF BOB by Caleb T. Brabham
Published by Creation House
A Strang Company
600 Rinehart Road
Lake Mary, Florida 32746
www.strangbookgroup.com

This is a work of fiction. Any resemblance to persons, places, or events is purely coincidental.

Design Director: Bill Johnson
Cover design by Justin Evans

Library of Congress Control Number: 2009937870
International Standard Book Number: 978-1-59979-967-4

10 11 12 13 — 9 8 7 6 5 4 3
Printed in the United States of America

In a style that is reminiscent of C. S. Lewis, this work displays thoughtful insights into theological and intellectual beliefs. Brabham utilizes skillfully humorous dialogue with a uniquely creative storyline to stir the reader's imagination and senses alike.

—RICK BURTON
FOUNDER/DIRECTOR, MUSTARD TREE MISSIONS

DEDICATION

To Judah, my brother.

And to Eric Tate, because faith is always rewarded.

CONTENTS

PROLOGUE

"**D**O YOU SEE THEM?" HE POINTED HIS FINGER toward the school in the depths of the glassy lake.

"The silver one with the red crest. That's the one. I'm going for him," Bob said.

"No, no. Drop the net around the school over there. You'll be sure to get them that way."

"I want a challenge. I've been chasing this one for six, or seven is it?" Bob insisted.

"Seven thousand years—you've been chasing him all week." He rose from the lake, His legs and the trim of His robe a wet sort of dry. Structurally, there was nothing about His face particularly distinctive. If He were anyone else, He might have been only described as youthful or handsome. But because He was Him, and only because, it could be said that just by smiling He was the Sun. And just by looking at you He could be your Best Friend.

The Shining Man, as He was the only source of light in this place, looked over His shoulder even though He didn't have to. The one who swore ever to hate Him and to deliver His destruction and who could truly be called the sorest loser of all was coming to whine to Him.

The whiner was covered in a robe from each country, each province, each city worldwide. They poured off of him, trailed after him, and made his appearance glorious in every place except this place. In this place, he was the dingiest rag in the Kingdom. Even he knew it. Every day his self-festooned glory reminded him of it.

Upon his head he wore a crown of masks, a veritable headdress of scales, feathers, and decorations. Each mask was another

1

emotion: hate, envy, lust, grief, regret, pain, fascination, depression, and one that seemed to resemble some form of happiness.

As he crept closer, he paused for a moment at the translucent pool. He reached his dirty claw into its pleasantly cool trappings. Long nails impaled one of the golden finned fishes; he lifted his masks and he placed it in his charred mouth. Fanged incisors bit the head of the flapping guppy, chewing the raw meat in a way that suggested mutilation more than it did mastication.

The Fish Eater looked to his Foe, crouched by Bob's side with His back to the Fish Eater. The Fish Eater had always thought, *If I could just sneak up behind Him, I could stab Him in the back.* And so he crept up as stealthily as he had taught the serpents and other quiet, deadly creatures.

He found himself facing The Shining Man. Not because He had turned, but because they were in another part of that world altogether, away from all the spectators.

"What is it, Lucifer?" He asked. "What makes it worth the trouble to come here?"

Shaken but unsurprised by the shift, The Fish Eater began, "Your man, the one You were with when I came—"

"I'm with all of my mothers and brothers here. I'm still with him right now," He said, drying His hands on His tunic. "But, yes, I know who you mean. He's out of your hands now."

"I just thought You'd like to know," The Fish Eater's slithery voice grew stronger as he raised his trump card, "that because of the cataclysm last week, the one that claimed Your man's life, I have coaxed a group of lowly vagabonds, some even once followers of You, to see this fellow as a god! Isn't that marvelous?" He cackled as if telling the best joke he ever heard.

"Do you think I didn't already know? I granted you permission to commit that deception three days ago. Did you just now get around to it?" Oddly, the Shining Man did not seem angered. He seemed quiet in His sorrowful disappointment in His foe. Not sorry for what His foe had perpetrated but for the way His foe was, or rather the way he chose to be.

"And I'm sure You know how I did it, with his very own book, the journal that he should've dedicated every last page to praising, glorifying, and worshiping Your precious—"

"Enough," He said, His quiet whisper putting a dead calm in the Fish Eater. "There is no condemnation for him here. I suggest you be about your way. And I will remind you, you do not have long."

The conversation ended and the Fish Eater stomped to his hole, all the while trying to convince himself that it was he who had won the argument.

By this time Bob had thrown the net in the crystal pool, and once again the clever fish dodged the net and scampered farther away from the school.

"Lord, I know it isn't important now, but how are things on Earth?" Bob asked.

The Shining Man put His thick carpenter's hands on Bob's shoulders. "I'm with them. There is no place, nowhere, that they are that I am not. I'm on every street corner, perched on every rooftop, and if they will let me, I'm holding every hand."

THE JOURNAL OF BOB

In this first entry, we get our only glimpse at our leader in his childhood. Humble even at his beginning, he resists his true calling, desiring instead a toy rocket ship, or perhaps even a real one, as it is never explicitly stated.

—BOBERT

Jan. 11th, first entry:

Hi. My name is Bob. I six year old. And I did not want a diary for Christmas. I want a rocketship.

Chapter 1

SUNSHINE ON MUSHROOM FLOWERS

One Week Ago

Steam slithered along the side of the bathtub while Sellia waltzed around her apartment. As she drifted she watched her reflection over the shimmering surfaces.

The television talked to her from the center of the room, vying in vain for her attention, "...morning...fighting erupted...leader ...peace promises...breakdown..."

She walked back to the bathroom, closing the door behind her, and paused at the counter to truly give herself a good appraisal. She was tanned to a chestnut brown. Her eyes pouted, then fluttered, then opened with amazement as they watched their own dance. Her blond hair with autumn colors was still precisely at shoulder length, and even without her morning shower was still soft and weightless. She puckered her lips, twisted them, sucked on them, and finally smiled. Her biggest concern was whether to brush her teeth first or step in the shower.

She chose the shower. With a metallic *whisk* the curtains opened and she stepped into the lathery steam of her cocoon. The hot water burned the morning chill away as she brushed her hair back into the showerhead's loving embrace.

A whistle. Faint, yet it seemed to rise up around her. Only the pipes. *Probably the Larabees downstairs,* she thought.

The noise. Boom or bang or roar; it was too loud to discern. The tiny room shook. Sellia slipped on the shower floor, thinking only that she was glad she did not bring the toothbrush in with her. Her one-track world went blank.

Today

The first sensation she felt was the cold enamel of the bathtub pressed against her skin. And then the stale leftover air that had been circulating until it had grown tired and sat on her back until she revived.

The water had stopped running, and now a tiny pool lay at the bottom underneath her. As she sat up, the dizziness soon came and pushed itself further into her brain as she tried to stand. Her eyes opened and shut but were only seeing a kaleidoscope of black, yellow, and green. Her bare feet stepped onto the linoleum of the bathroom floor. With her hands feeling the walls desperately, she walked into the sitting room.

When her eyes finally began taking in their surroundings, they saw dust and smoke floating in the spectrum of frozen light coming through the window. Glass was upon the floor, as were branches, dirt, and a tiny bird.

He was resting on his wing, with his brown speckled head jutting forward and his claws cocked. He squinted in eternal concentration. Sellia cringed at the sight of it. She could only imagine the maggots would find him soon. She could feel the invisible germs of death crawl off of it and onto her. She reached her arms up and clutched herself, trying to halt the ripple of shivers through her skin. She quickly sidestepped the shards of glass and fled to her closet, all the while feeling the stare of its clenched eyes.

At her closet a pair of worn and friendly jeans smiled at her through the holes in their knees. She fooled herself for a moment, thinking she would put them on in order to visit the outside, but then she caught the glance of her short cotton dress, white and blameless, sashaying in the breeze offered by the broken window. She remembered that she would at least see the bellboy and possibly her neighbor down the hall with the square jaw. She grabbed it, pulling it on over her head. It caught her tangled hair as it went down. As it produced the neckline, Sellia giggled as its scratchy fibers tickled her skin. With a smooth gesture, she ran her fingers down her hips, adjusting the dress and straitening the fibers. She flipped her hair to seduce the mirror, the dried clunky mass of hair hanging heavy from her scalp. It was an emergency that deserved her immediate coddling.

Sellia marched back across the floor of her apartment to the bathroom, leaping across the glass and inadvertently kicking the bird away from her path. In the bathroom, she plucked clamps and bows to tuck and hold her hair back, using various seconds to make it appear as though she had spent hours doing her hair.

From her purse hanging by the door, Sellia withdrew her lipstick and makeup. She took another few moments spackling and toning and dusting, once again creating the miracle of appearing as if she not only spent hours to look as a goddess, but that she woke up early to do so.

She stood in front of the image of reflected elegance that was framed upon her bathroom wall over her sink. Her skin, flawless. Her hair, favorable. Her dress? She was attempting to think of a better word than *sultry*, but couldn't.

She was ready.

Unlocking her door and snagging her pearl pumps, she bounded out of the room, even spinning a little as she snuck a look over her shrugged shoulder. The hallway was a horizontal abyss with plush carpeting, lit only through the window from Sellia's apartment and provided ably by the door that was still ajar.

She leaned toward the floor and tugged the pumps onto her feet. Her tongue massaged her back two teeth as she mentally searched her room for a flashlight. Remembering none and impatient to venture downward to her city, she pranced into the blackness. Instinctively finding her way to the stairs, she gripped the railing, preparing for her blind descent.

One, two, three, Sellia was thinking, *fourteen steps till the landing. Four, five, six... is it really fourteen? Did I ever count them? It's probably fifteen. That's nice and round. But it's an odd number. I wonder if most stairs are built even or odd.*

Barely grazing the seventh step on the fourteen-step staircase—or was it fifteen?—one of the gaunt high heels snapped, careening her toward the landing. Even the soft carpet could not cushion the fall or stop the resulting sting from the crash. Sellia buried her face in its cotton tendrils. She gritted her teeth, gnawing on them. Angry, she sat up on her knuckles, arching her back into feline form, ready to pounce.

And then she spotted the luminous trail of the lobby doorway. Quickly, she gathered herself and cleared the rest of the stairs as if they were less than a thought. She turned her head and shot a heart-enslaving glance outside and saw...

Gray. As Sellia walked through the downtrodden city streets, slick with the sweat of humidity, she noticed that the raised side-walks, toppled buildings, submerged cars, and unearthed water mains all had that one thing in particular in common. The chalky tint shaded them all. Clouds hung especially low, dragging the nebulous, gray, ashen mass. The newly formed rivers were parched with the dust as they flowed like sap in the cavernous asphalt basin. The only color came from her tear-stained, bloodshot eyes.

She had arrived fashionably late on the scene, as was her usual custom. And in keeping with her other usual custom, her cotton, white dress matched the occasion, if she was not just a bit overdressed.

"Hello!" she yelled. "What happened? Is anyone out there?" She gawked at her surroundings and her old haunts, from Narcissi Plaza to the Charlatan Hotel. With windows shattered, they stared back with sunken eyes like some of her old friends she had forsaken because they had lost their charm.

With no destination in her mind, her feet carried her to the duck pond, down the wickedly curving street. Her other high heel broke off in one of the ripples of the concrete as she tried to descend to the fog-encased bank. Regardless, Sellia kept both shoes on as she tried to hold her nose during her approach to the shoreline. Fish dotted the ground, and with their half smiles they stared back at her. She tried to avert her eyes. But still she wandered to the bank, with her broken pearl pumps adorning themselves in mud with every step.

And then she froze. On a tilted, sandblasted bench a man lay with a blue fedora covering his face. He wore the latest styles of a muddy, untucked shirt and torn or burned pinstripe slacks. Too stylish for shoes, he wore none.

"Oh! I'm so glad to see somebody! Can you tell me what happened?" She stumbled as she ran to him. He did not stir. She slowed down her pace to a goopy trot as she asked, "Are you all right? Please tell me you can hear me." His pale skin seemed dusty from the fallout, and his black, curly hair had traces of dirt and pebbles in its tangles. *If he has been here long,* she thought, *chances are he's...*

"Why?" she yelled, pitching a fit, boiling the mud with her temper. She kicked the bench with all her might, knocking it completely over and sending the young man spiraling onto the muddy turf.

He grunted, bracing his hands wrist deep in the powdery slop.

"Oh my! You're alive? I'm so sorry," Sellia apologized. He ignored her as he tried to dig himself out of his foxhole.

"Uh, hello? Um, are you mad at me?" Sellia said. Suddenly, he stood up and looked her in the chin, the full extent of his height. "Oh, hello. I didn't know you were there."

Sellia gaped to see the headphones in his ears connecting with a dusty CD player. He removed it. She could almost hear the chorus of a song she could not place. "Can I get back to you in a few minutes? I only have about ten more minutes of battery life and this is my favorite part." He wiped his hands on his trousers before picking up his hat and strolling off. He bobbed to his music, his gait swerving as he hummed along.

Sellia's bottom lip puckered. "I, uh... There's no one, nothing here, and you want to listen to... to music?"

But he could not hear her. She looked around. Maybe there would be someone elsewhere. Following the instinct that had carried her thus far, she trudged on toward the rest of the city. She passed him with her nose turned upward as she defiantly marched in her search for life. "Crazy," she said to herself.

She took about ten paces toward The Grand Palisade Theatre, a block east of the pond, where every Saturday night at eight o'clock a box was reserved for her in the name of one desperate or jealous suitor or another. So many lost weekends had been spent there as of late that she had nicknamed all the ushers and had been glad-handed by the owner as a cherished patron, though she had gotten in free each night.

She awoke from her trance as the young man from the bench grasped her shoulder. "You don't need to go that way."

"And why not? A dozen of them there are at my beck and call every night when there is no danger at all. Just think of how they'll want to help me when the city looks like this."

He turned off his CD player and laid it on the ground, perfectly content that no one would pick it up. "Even so, I would recommend you stay here."

"Why? Do you have a plan for rescue? Have you seen anybody?" Sellia asked.

"Technically, yes," he said steadily, his eyes averting to the sky, chasing a glimpse of sun.

"Yet you're content to sit here and listen to music and starve? Well, I'm famished, and I haven't touched a bite since before whatever happened, happened."

He grabbed her wrist. "I never said I didn't have a plan."

"Will you let go?" she said, her dazzling white eyes cutting like beacons through the smog.

He released, resigning himself to silence. He slipped his hands in his pockets as he looked toward the dim horizon, away from Sellia as she walked toward The Palisade.

She could barely keep her eyes from watering as she approached the old theater. For its half-century of existence, it never seemed to show even the first moment of age, but in a single day it looked no different from any other crumbling ancient edifice. She tried to smile the same plastic grin she wore every weekend as she approached the box office, but when she saw that one of the columns had snapped backward and crashed through the ticket window, the smile faded. And as she looked inside the bloodied booth, her knees buckled, sending her in a spiraling descent to the craggy, dusty, glass-splintered, gravel pavement. She only heard the gallop of the young man's feet as she lay there.

"No one survived. I mean, well, you're the only other one I've seen so far," he said.

Her eyes slammed shut as her mouth stretched into a wide, toothy frown and she began to wail.

"It's...it's not that bad. I mean, I can look after you for a while until we find a rescue party."

She stopped crying long enough to look at his cherub-like, dust-covered features and the ridiculous hat balancing lopsidedly on his head. She cried louder.

"I mean, there's plenty of food here, canned goods in the grocery stores. I'm sure we can even have a hot meal if we can figure out how to make a fire. Maybe that fish is good."

Her eyes opened long enough to give him a look of death as she whined, shaking her head in the messy street.

"OK, we'll work up to that. But if we leave it out too long it'll spoil," he said.

She sat up. "Take a big whiff. What does that smell like to you?" she asked. They both looked in the general direction of the pond. Its perfumed essence had lingered over to them as if it were the third member of their party, running after them and yelling, "Wait for me, wait for me!"

"Now, what's *that* smell?" Sellia asked.

"I don't smell anything."

She leaned closer to him and sniffed around his collar. Her head jerked back in a show of repulsion. "What is that foul musk?"

His bushy eyebrows rippled and arched, he, too, apparently disgusted. "That's my cologne. My favorite cologne. My *lucky* cologne," he announced. "I'll have you know I got my first kiss wearing this cologne."

"And how many years ago was that?"

"About ten or twelve."

She stood up, vainly dusting herself off. "I think it's about time for a change. You know, every six months or three thousand miles."

He shrugged his shoulders. "Anyway, I never got your name."

"Sellia," she replied, looking away seemingly disinterested at whether or not she received his.

"I'm Sam."

"I know a lot of Sams," she said sourly.

"There's a very easy way you can remember my name. It's a song:

Sammy boy, Oh, Sammy boy,
He's the ladies' pride and joy.
That's why they act so coy.
Just to see their Sammy boy
Sammy—

"OK, OK, that's enough," she said as the moderate distaste in her eyes showed, and she added, "You think that up all by yourself?"

"I had a little help from another Sam."

"Oh, good." She began walking off on her own again.

"Uh," he said grimacing, "that's not a good idea."

She stopped. "Oh, right. Don't want to see any more of that again. Where are we going?"

"My place," Sam pointed down the crackled pavement to a tucked-away staircase beneath a crumbled edifice. The tiny stairs led below the pavement to an abandoned basement studio. As he guided her down the steps, Sellia could not take her eyes off of the humbled city, with its knees firmly set in the ground. She looked down in time to see Sam shove open the door. Judging from the bit of molding and frame that were still stuck to the padlock, it did not appear that Sam owned the place.

THE JOURNAL OF BOB

This proverb is found only a few pages after the first entry, but it is apparent that the scribe wrote this passage at least a decade afterward.

—BOBERT

Excerpt from Feb. 12th entry:

A king of hearts and a queen of diamonds do not help make a full house.

Chapter 2

KING AND QUEEN

SAM'S MAKESHIFT HOME HAD THE SAME CHARM as the place underneath a rug where dust has been swept. The old dance studio, replete with crooked, fallen pictures of jazz singers, looked like it had been done in long before the catastrophe. Full posters illustrating the dance steps of the foxtrot and the turkey hop littered the floor.

"What happened?" asked Sellia.

"You know, a little neglect, a little—"

"No, I meant to the city. It was so beautiful yesterday. But, this morning I woke up on the floor of...my apartment."

"Which apartment?"

"Hartleton Suites."

"You think you slept through it?" he asked, surprised. "It's been like this the past three days, unless it did a number on my memory, too."

"What?"

"That must'a been *some* sleep. You must've been knocked out by some of the debris."

Her eyes were swollen, seemingly even more depressed at this than the loss of the city. "I lost three days?"

"Do you want soup or ravioli?" With a flick of his wrist, he unveiled a turret of cans, obviously built to defend against starvation.

"I want my days back," she said, holding her jaw in her hands as her nails delicately tapped her face. Sam turned to look her over. Her face did not flinch, her eyes did not overflow with tears, but her little ceramic world was spilled out for only him to see.

In a fluid moment, she vanished from the room, standing and

excusing herself faster than Sam could stop her, running harder in broken high heels than any jogger she ever scoffed at from the peaks of her loft. She tripped up the stairs and onto the wilderness plain, blindly watching the horizon as she ran, giving in to her anxious instincts desperate to lead her on a tour of this cowering new world. Sweet and unrelenting, the slow string of nostalgia tugged her to her place of constant surrender, of nagging desire—the Bethesda Pines Outlet Mall.

Always white, the colors never faded, even in the wake of the disaster. If anything, the caking, snowy powder brought out a certain visceral whimsy that the market never had before. A red carpet of cracked glass had been laid out in expectation for Queen Sellia. Handsome and dainty mannequins bowed and curtseyed for her majesty as she walked into the first store, which had been spared a cave-in. The merchandise seemed grateful not to be asked to give in to the sufferings of the other shops.

"Don't you look darrrrling!" Sellia said, grabbing a yellow gown. She leapt across the hallway to the jewelry boutique and began adorning herself with rings, bracelets, and necklaces until her fingers could not wiggle, her arms could not sway, and her neck could not support her head.

She began trading her mud-stained clothing for the gown, her sullied soles for shiny slippers, and all the essential decorum that every Sellia must own. She held her nose high and marched to the nearest mirror. Cracked and shattered as it was, it was still truthful, showing her dried hair tangled and ragged, though hidden and tucked through clips and ribbons. She could feel her scalp itch from the dirt and grime of three days without a rinse.

"Disgusting!" she reeled. "My hair! I'll have to fix it."

She sashayed to the salon and helped herself to shampoos, conditioners, and a spare towel from the back. With a satisfied smile she turned her attention to the sink. She delicately turned the knob a quarter turn. No water. She turned it a full turn. No water.

"How dare you," she seethed through clenched teeth. She hugged her items to her and waltzed outside the mall to the lake. Her world, her domain, still looked the same. But as she floated in her radiant yellow gown, it was clear what was different. She had become royalty in a single day.

Beside the pond, she rolled up her dress and plopped to her knees, pulling her hair free from its accessories. Sellia dipped her blonde hair in the still water.

"Excuse me!" A booming voice came from the shadowy world above the bubbles.

"Stop her! She's drowning herself!" another said. Plastic arms pulled her out of peril.

"What do you bandits want?" she gasped as dirty water trickled down her face. Her intruders stared at her through black masks that seemed to hide all but their eyes while troubling their breathing. "You could've cleaned yourselves up before presenting yourselves to a lady," she said, undaunted, and pointing to their dust-covered black and yellow robes.

The men exchanged bewildered looks with each other through their breathing apparati.

"What's your name, miss?" a blue-eyed bandit asked her.

"Sammy boy, Sammy boy...something, something, pride and joy," she whispered.

"Ma'am?" he asked again.

"This one's in shock," said another. "Get ready to carry her back."

Two of the bandits grabbed her and began trying to carry her off to their flaming fire-engine spaceship festooned in bulbous flashing red and yellow lights.

"No!" Sellia yelled. "Let go. You can't take me away from my home. You can't. I won't let you." She wriggled in their plastic, inhuman arms. Pulling left and right, up and down, she collapsed and yielded to her last resort. And with sadly sullen eyes she humbled herself and yelled, "Sam! Sam, help! I need you."

Like a film noir cavalryman, Sam came running out of his hideout. Reaching into his pocket, he pulled out his prized lucky cologne and hurled it into the fray. The golden vial twirled in a dazzling arc and smashed in the face of an unhappy bandit. Sellia hit the charred landscape a second later, wiggling on her belly toward Sam through the forest of stocky legs.

Sam gave her his hand and helped her to her feet. "Are you OK?"

"Look at my dress!" She cocked her head, "There's dust all over it now."

"Let's get out of here." He tugged her arm and the king and queen of the city ran together toward the shelter of swaggering buildings under the smoggy, soot-filled sunset.

THE JOURNAL OF BOB

This is the passage where we get our mandate for behavior. When Bob was fifteen, a higher power bestowed these rules upon him. It is not explicitly stated what this authority was. But it is fairly implied that it is a Spirit or Deity. Perhaps even more likely, because there is no figure stated, these rules were created by Bob to better himself. In his humility, he made sure to never attribute the list to himself. Though Bob at first seems reluctant to comply, his compliance shaped the shining example that he eventually became.

—BOBERT

Excerpt from Aug. 13th entry: six months from previous entry

Because of last night, I heard just now the rules I am supposed follow.

I have to be home by nine most nights and in bed by ten.

I can't go out with my friends

...or date without a chaperone...ever...for now.

I can't watch TV.

I am not allowed to finish my book, 'Chauncey Pepper and the Sixteenth Way Home,' which is stupid because Pepper and his buddies just discovered that Sissie is employed by The Vanguard and has been since book four.

I don't know how long this is for, but I hope it's not long.

Chapter 3

MOSES

THE BLOOD RED LIGHTS OF THE CHARIOT SWELLED in the alleyway. It embraced them as they refused and struggled to be free of it. The red was as impossibly scary as a carnal fear that clung to the ribs, as the glare shunned and beckoned at once.

"I take it you know where you're taking us," Sellia said as she looked to Sam, his bare feet pattering before her through the coals of stone, becoming black with each step. In her new heels and with the weight of her jewelry, she struggled to keep the pace.

Sam did not answer her as he continued running, seemingly trying to gauge it so as not to leave her behind. One turned corner after another revealed another pile of building and another puddle of skyscraper.

When he stopped, Sellia peered into those cherub eyes waiting for her. "Where are we going?" she asked. The clump-clump-clump of thick boots could be heard as the bandits followed their footprints through the snowy ash.

"Quick, hide," he said, removing his fedora and tossing it to a corner, now scarlet in the glowing light. Sam dove into the blanket of ash of a bowing building, dragging her body in with him. The enormous ashdrift devoured them, burping a cloud of remembrance into the alley beyond them.

The dust stung her already dry, watery eyes. *Stupid Sam,* she thought, *I have to make a dramatic point. Cares more about that stupid hat than*—and then she heard them. In spite of the soot filling her ear like a funnel, she heard them, mostly.

"You say…this way?" one bandit said. "They've already gone through…when you find them," another said. When the alley was unearthly silent once more, the two royals unearthed themselves from their borough.

"They don't seem so bad," said Sam, heaving dust, ignoring the suggesting quiet from the alley as he dragged himself away from the pile. Sellia, with her arm to her mouth, attempted to muffle her cough. Vainly, she tried to swat at Sam in a reproach for being so loud.

Then suddenly the bandits called out, "What's that? Hey, hey guys! They're over here!"

Sam had just been able to lift himself to his knees before Sellia grabbed his limp shirt collar. "C'mon!" she yelled.

"I don't know," he said, his tongue caked with dirt, "if it isn't such a good idea if we let them catch us."

"Bandits are pillaging our home. You want to let them catch us? On second thought, why don't you protect us from them? Why don't you fight them, huh?"

With eyes equally as bloodshot as hers, he stared back in fury. He grabbed her frail little hand so newly reacquainted with dirt, and ran back the way they came, away from the echoing clatter of bandits.

Once in the street, he craned his long neck in elliptical arcs. To the north, the city appeared as if it had slowly tipped into the ocean. Almost every building seemed to wade up to their rooftops in the sludge.

He continued running, dragging Sellia and her burning lungs behind him like a puppy dog's tail until he reached North Edict Street's aquarium, a building that looked more like a bunker due to its blocky concrete structure. Sam led her through the metallic doors with bronzed dolphin imprints. Though the building stood mostly intact, the inside hallways had not been spared the deluge. Fish, far more colorful this time, spackled the tile.

"What is it with you and fish?" Sellia asked in disgust.

Still remorseful over losing his hat he said, "I'm *helping you*—the least you could do is be less picky of our hideout." He turned toward a gold railing and followed it to the next level, where a catwalk led to the next room. The treadless catwalk swam in the light offered by an enormous and cracked aquarium still filled with water…and something else.

Its monstrous shape fell over Sellia and covered her in its dingy shadow. She gasped. Sam looked over his shoulder only to make sure her knees had not buckled again. It was an object so large it defied life, shattering the mind's ability to conceive a creature of such size able to sustain itself. It boasted its twenty-foot-long coils in wiggles and squiggles, stretched across the beast's transparent home. So reptilian was its snout and pointy teeth, it was difficult to comprehend its ten fins, which propelled it in buzzard-like circles behind the glass.

"It's a dinosaur!" she yelped in a swallowed scream.

"It's still a fish," Sam corrected, looking at a plaque on the wall that indicated the scientific name of the beast. "*Atractosteus spatula*," Sam read, and tugged on the colorful sticky tab applied next to the bronze. "Its name is Old Moses. It'll be sixteen in December."

A leviathan from a Hobbesian hell, Moses looked at them from its glass prison through membranous eyes. It smiled, each tooth as large as a human head. The teeth were barbed and trenchant in their cut, as if they too had been forged in the blast furnace with Dame Justice's sword and scales in order to become just another instrument of annihilation, a bowl of nihilistic judgment.

Her hand once more covering her mouth in reverence of the hideous and horrible happenstance, Sellia turned and ran up the golden-rimmed staircase. She drove her heels into the tile staircase repeating over and over to her fear, "I'm not listening. You can't reach me. I'm safe—I'm safe!"

As she stumbled onto the top floor, she saw Moses' promised land. The aquarium stretched to the back of the building where a wall had crumbled, uniting Moses with the flooded back lot. With its fins it swaggered by, as if meeting the two was merely a courtesy.

"Sam! Tap the glass! Get its attention!"

"What?"

"There's a hole in the back of the aquarium! It can get out!"

Obediently, Sam hit the glass. Moses was not disturbed or dissuaded. Sam began to beat a rhythm on the aquarium. Sellia could almost feel the continuous vibrations as she overlooked the open pool. The water wiggled as Old Moses turned toward the disruption. It lingered nearer, tugging its fellows, pain and punishment, with it. With every flick of its sinuous fins, it sent water trickling down the sides of the crumbling aquarium, through the growing crack.

She saw the slice in the glass searing like jagged lightning toward Sam's dusty head as fast as the ensuing reptilian smile. Immediately, her mind brought up a dozen gruesome scenarios, many of them stemming from bloody scenes she had witnessed inside the box office. Her lips moved, but her voice did not. Sam, only encouraged by the coming of Old Moses, continued pounding. She tried again, only managing a wet cough and a gurgle deep inside her throat. She pictured Sam on the bench in that droopy fedora he tossed aside to help her. She first thought he was dead. That fedora. He could not live without it. He very well could not have left the earth without it.

"Sam! Stop!" she screamed.

In mid-beat, he dropped his fist and looked up to her. He looked back, and with horror registered the splitting seams of glass above him. Sam backed away and up the steps after her voice. Old Moses, having lost its focus, drifted off in its wistful, watery slither toward the open world, and with the recoil of the waves, floated out.

Sellia was still watching the ripples in the empty tank when Sam came up behind her.

"Thanks," he whispered.

Shutting her eyes, and without acknowledging his words, she manipulated her stilted feet toward a corridor of aquariums containing much smaller fish.

THE JOURNAL OF BOB

This is the first instance of the character of Melvin. He seems to be the Enkidu to Bob's Gilgamesh. In this excerpt, we see their interaction over the task of fishing. It is important to gather the yin and yang qualities of these characters. Where Bob is peace, Melvin is force. They are not opposing; they are complimentary.

—BOBERT

Entry from April 14th: seven years from previous entry

Today, Melvin and I took our Bowmaster 2000 out on the lake. We were still determined to catch something. Melvin assured me that today was the day.

I wasn't as confident. Melvin spent most of the time leaning against the stern neglecting his rod and reel. He told me that this was part of his plan.

Taking his rest for complacency, I concentrated on catching our fish. But he must've been more alert than I was because the next thing I knew Melvin was yelling at me that I had a bite.

As I began tugging the pole with all my might, Melvin dove into a box at the back of the boat. Melvin came back shouldering a rifle and firing repetitively in the water.

We caught the fish, but as I cleaned him that night, picking bullet fragments from among the scales, it felt more like I was doing an autopsy.

Chapter 4

WEST SIDE BRIDGE

"**D**ID YOU HEAR ME?" SAM ASKED. "I DIDN'T REALIZE the glass was breaking. Phew, I'd hate to think what would've happened."

Sellia's attention was disembodied now, once again lost in the trance of destruction. Her body swayed and sashayed through the hall of amber tanks of dead fish, crystallized in their own waste. She was being pulled and tugged and led through to the end of the hallway where a gleaming white window to the outside beckoned.

With the delicacy of a china doll's hand, Sellia stroked the glass of the window and peered out upon her city's smoky countenance. On the other side of the river, towers stood as giants with shimmering crowns. Sellia licked her lips at the sight of those gems. A bridge of chrome and steel cross-sections speckled with wire hugged the two urban landmasses together.

"What's that?" her voice cracked the silence. "The bridge is still standing?"

"That's the West Erickson Bridge."

"I know what it is! Why is it still standing?"

"Why are you still alive? Why am I? Why are we still here, how do we know if we really are—?"

"I asked you a question, Nietzsche! Stop philosophizing!"

"Technically, it's more Descartes. Why are you so interested?"

"There are lights on over there. The bridge connects to another city, and they have their lights on!"

"It's still the same city," Sam reminded her.

"There must be people over there!"

"Maybe. Are you saying you want to go?"

Sellia skipped down the hallway of embalmed fish to the golden-rimmed staircase.

"Wait, Sellia! Don't you know they'll be waiting for you?"

Disobedient and determined, Sellia continued her queen's waltz to the foyer of her aquatic palace. Once at the door, she peered into the streets before dashing west.

Destiny, desire, ownership. *This city is mine,* Sellia thought. *Whose city is that? Surely, if they have lights, the queen doesn't march the streets like a commoner there. Nor do bandits assault her. What will she do when she sees me? Surely, she will despise me for my appearance. I hate you for that, Sam. Ruining my first impression with fellow royalty.* Her desires, sweet and unrelenting, pulled her with compelling interest toward the West Side Bridge.

Suddenly, like an eggshell on a kitchen floor, so unwanted and so out of place, Sellia saw the inhuman, masked bandit standing guard on the West Erickson Bridge. His bulbous eyes and nozzle nose tilted away, she knew she could look at him without fear. She analyzed his appearance, his shinning head, which jutted back toward the bridge.

The arrogance! The impudence! *How could he think he could block the path of a queen,* she thought. With enough resolve to dilute a flask of acid, she marched toward the stalwart soldier.

Two burly arms encased her and lifted her away from the ground. So sudden was this transition that as she was carried away, her feet briefly continued the motion of walking. The arms took her from the bridge through alleys until they entered a white, soot-covered office building, eclipsed from the gaze of the bandits.

"Confound you, Sam! Why can't you leave me alone when I'm trying to—"

"Shhhhhhh," was the surrounding reply from the gallery of plain-clothed folk.

The burly-armed man who had grabbed her was twice Sam's height and build. His smile was a mangled smirk: crooked and lopsided. His immense posture folded and reclined while standing. He wore a bright yellow, translucent poncho with its hood back. About his body there was a smell, a distinct odor of something that should be alive but wasn't.

He addressed her, "Who are you, girl?"

"You incompetent goof! You stopped me from—"

"I saved you from being taken to wherever they're taking the survivors," Burly Arms said. "Probably some monitoring station to make sure they're not radioactive or whatever," he turned to the others. "And if we're going to die, we're going to do it here!"

"Good Times," the group replied.

"I want to go to the West Side," Sellia insisted, swatting the air in front of her.

"I do too, sister," an old woman said. Coming up to Sellia's shoulders, the old woman was clearly the shortest in the group. "My grandbaby's over there."

"Does she have the mark? The red streak?" a black-haired woman asked.

"Yes, did you check for the red streak?" a scrawny teen asked.

"The fire-men won't let you pass. The West Side is restricted. Maybe a quarantine. I'm not sure," Burly Arms said. Then in an aside to the rest, he said, "And that was the first thing I checked. No."

"Good Times," the group chanted, scratching their bowed heads in identical motions.

"Is there any other way to get to the West Side?" Sellia asked.

"Why worry about the West Side? This is where was chosen for us," Burly Arms stated affirmatively. "We were placed here, ordained to meet and live in concordance and harmony."

"Good Times!" they chanted in synchronization.

She could not ignore it anymore. "OK, what is going on around here?" Sellia asked.

Burly Arms bowed slightly, mangling his smile even more. "I am but a humble servant. I changed my real name to better follow our leader, the one who wrote this book. I changed mine to his."

An older gentleman from the crowd sporting thick, worn glasses and a graying comb-over carried a medium sized leather-bound journal. He opened it to her, revealing the name.

"Bob?" Sellia asked.

The followers all spat.

"Don't speak his name," the burly armed prophet said, pointing his finger at her. He was almost emotionless. But the cold way he executed the gesture and the breathless atmosphere it created from his congregants suggested to Sellia his own violent disgust.

"But I thought your name was—"

"That's different. My name is our leader's name spelled backward: boB."

"Good Times," the followers said.

"Now comes the important part. Will you join us, girl?" boB asked.

"Pssst," came from the doorway.

As Sellia turned her head, she drew the attention of the congregation to Sam clinging to the shadows.

"Ding dong?" Sam inquired sheepishly, walking into the fellowship.

"Howdy, stranger!" The scrawny teen approached Sam. Sellia noticed her first judgments on Sam's stature were harsh. Next to this young man, Sam was filled out and muscular. Next to boB, Sam's posture was confident and perfect. "Another convert!" the teen said. Sam's eyes reared back in shock as the shaggy-haired, chicken-boned teen slapped him on the back.

"What a sweet face. Cherub eyes, too," the old woman said as she stroked Sam's face and pulled him into an embrace.

"Got nothing on boB," a young lady with long black hair said in disgust. She batted her eyes at an oblivious boB.

"Thanks, I got them from…my…mother. Yeah!" Sam tried not to be eager as he attempted to walk away from his greeters. He cleared the first fifty feet of the office building's reception room over to Sellia in two strides.

"Sellia, what is this?" Sam asked, his voice cracking, his eyes warily darting about the room.

"This," boB said not unceremoniously, "is a place for survivors. We don't need to follow the scared and confused fire-men leading people away from the city. Instead of trying to fix its problems, they just give up and run away. If you want to solve problems, you start here with us, friend." He paced as he spoke. This, combined with his soft, grumbling voice, made him seem like a great predatory cat. Presently, his head tilted back as if Sam displeased him.

"I'm just following her. I didn't know there were any other survivors," Sam said.

boB smirked as he continued his methodical walk. "Yes, there are more people in the world than just yourself." It was obvious now that boB was walking to what had been the secretary's desk. He slouched into a thickly padded leather executive chair that both conspicuously and unsuccessfully hid behind the tiny desk.

"I've only had a few seconds' head start. But just do what I do," Sellia whispered before turning to boB and his congregation. "I accept. I want to be a part of your fellowship."

"And you. You, too, accept?" boB asked.

"Uh, yeah. Yeah, I do," Sam said.

"He doesn't seem to be that interested. I don't think he'll be that true to our cause," black-haired lady said. "He only wants the girl."

"Whatever has brought him here, he will stay and hear our message. Which is cool," Bobert said.

Sam thought for a second, then caught Sellia's lips moving in the corner of his eyes. A closer inspection, a stutter and a stammer later, and Sam said, "Good Times."

The congregation embraced him as one of their own.

THE JOURNAL OF BOB

This entry begins one of the most interesting parables of Bob's life, dealing specifically with his opposing entity, Wallace, and the character that seems to represent the unguided, Meredith.

Much can be derived from its meaning. The prose here would suggest that the red stripe against her white hair represents Meredith's inequity, or possibly more specifically, the inequity of those lost without Bob.

—BOBERT

Excerpt from May 15th: three months prior to previous entry

Archer's department store has kinda become my home away from home. I keep joking with Jon that I should put a cot back in one of the dressing rooms.

It's been ok working in the Bethesda Pines Mall. I go to the food court everyday. I think they're actually getting tired of seeing me there. Yesterday, the cashier at Digby's had my order ready before I even placed it.

Likewise the video and bookstores, who now know me by sight. At least they give me a discount when they see my tie and bright green Archer's nametag.

I guess one of the neat things is in working in a place that's so big. There are so many people around. I guess it's nice to know we're not outnumbered by the customers too badly.

But not everything is customer service and restocking. We're kind of one big dysfunctional family, complete with our own black sheep.

There's Wallace, our manager. He always seems

as if he's in a perpetual deadlock with corporate or buried in restocking orders. He also has a way with customers, always remembering their names, the health of their family members, and quite often their marital status. It is not uncommon to see him with a customer who had been in the store earlier that week. He would walk around 'on patrol' every few hours, giving us in depth tips on how to be better salesmen.

Jon works in men's clothing, right beside my shoe department, and is steadily becoming a friend of mine. It almost seems like Wallace has it out for him, often singling him out for special assignments, like staying 'til three in the morning to check in new shipments. Jon's been known to take advantage of our friendship on occasion, asking if I'll help receive. But despite that, I still think he's cool.

(...)

Then there's Meredith. She works at a counter in perfume over in the women's section. Hemmed blond hair with a dyed streak of red down the back. Watching her from behind, you have to shake the impulse that she's bleeding. We've only spoken a few times. Her voice is a pesky one. Not that it's husky, or loud, or a bad accent. It starts out pleasant enough, then it pitches upward so much so that you can almost see it drawn out like a line graph for the stock exchange. I don't like her...

Chapter 5

THE FOLLOWERS OF BOB

"**O**K, DAVE. WHAT DO YOU THINK THAT ONE IS?"

"You know? I don't know which one you're talking about."

"That one!" Bob pointed. "That cloud right over Missouri."

Bob, King David, Abraham, Adam, and Peter lay underneath one of heaven's mustard trees and watched the earth float through the cosmos beneath them.

"This makes me woozy," Peter said.

"Missouri?" David asked.

"I think it looks like a kangaroo. You know, hopping," Adam said.

"I see it!" someone shouted. All five of them looked up. It was Noah. "What're you guys doing?"

"Stuff," Adam said.

"Oh, OK," Noah said dejectedly as he walked away.

"Why'd you send him away?" Bob asked.

"Well, he's only good company if you talk to him about animals," Adam said.

The rest just stared at him for a long moment.

"I talk about other things!" Adam insisted.

"Yeah, I got a question for you, Adam," Bob started. "What was the deal about Cain marrying? I mean, who else was around?"

"Uh-oh," Abraham intervened. "We forgot to tell you the rules. If you're going to ask questions, we get to ask questions."

"Like what? What could you know about me?"

"We get to cheer you on, remember?" Abraham said

"And there were times, Bob, when it wasn't pretty," David said, wincing.

"Guns in your fishing boat, though, that was...*that* was something else!" Peter said.

"You guys are kinda mean, not like I pictured at all. Not half as uplifting," Bob said.

"Uh-oh," Adam said, his brow rising, an alarmed look grazing his face.

"It's Ol' Fish Eater again," Peter said resolutely as he looked at David. David nodded. The two got up and stood vigilantly.

"What? Who are they talking about?" Bob asked.

"It's the devil," Abraham said. "He can come up here, pretty much as he pleases. But he never likes to stay long."

"He doesn't like heaven?" Bob said.

"He can't stand being around Yahweh," Abraham smiled.

"Whenever he's around, things get a tiny bit less holy," Adam said. "For us, anyway."

"But that's why Jesus is going to make a new heaven and even a new Earth that's untouched by The Fish Eater," Peter said confidently.

"Bob." It was The Shining Man in a voice so warm, so loving, and so powerful, it startled the former shoe salesman.

"Yes, Lord," Bob said.

"Could you come here for a moment? I want you to see something."

"Of course." The Shining Man took Bob, and at once they were alone in another part of heaven and graced by the presence of The Fish Eater.

"Remember through this, he won't be able to see you," The Shining Man said.

"OK," Bob said steadily. He looked for the first time on the devil he had heard so much about. He was not red at all. And even though he was covered from head to toe in garments, Bob still searched fruitlessly for a pointed tail. Bob considered The Fish Eater's physical appearance. He knew the masks were scary and the gems were bright and the jewelry was ornate and that the garments were beautiful, but he didn't feel it. Nor did his heart agree with it.

"Yes, Lucifer. What is it?" The Shining Man said.

"I have it all together. All the players are in place. The Bobbers—Isn't that a clever name?—are about to have a feast in honor of their leader, Bob."

"Huh?" Bob said. "He doesn't mean—"

"I know," The Shining Man said.

"But look at them. Look at how the whole celebration detracts from You."

The Shining Man almost yawned. "Is that all?"

The Fish Eater became defensive. "At least watch!"

"I've already seen it before, but yes, let's go ahead and watch."

The Fish Eater opened his cloak and black smoke poured into the heavens. The smog swirled into a vortex and a window opened to Earth.

On Earth

The office building's conference room became the Bobbers' meeting hall; candlelight gave the closed, windowless quarters a clandestine atmosphere. Shadows lurked on the plaster walls. Sellia began to think that this place would look a lot less creepy with the florescent lights on.

boB settled in at the head of the table. As he passed by the candles, the glow of each made his yellow poncho shimmer and gave him the false radiance a stolen halo. His body appeared to be aflame with holy light, though his face was crossed with shadow that made his mangled smirk to appear all the more sinister.

"What are you serving, Mr. Bobert, our most holy scribe?" boB asked.

The man with the thick glasses and comb-over walked to his leader and tilted a cardboard box toward him. Bobert wore gray sweats with a hood open in back.

"Aha! Today we have been provided with industrial potted meat!" boB exclaimed heartily.

"Good Times!" the Bobbers chanted back.

boB turned to Sellia. "Would you like to be the first to taste this provision, girl?"

Sellia did not feel like opening her mouth for the mention of the food, much less answering to going first.

Sam took a seat beside her and spoke in her stead, "Could I go first? I mean, if Sellia doesn't mind?"

Sellia's eyes widened in thankfulness and nodded her approval to Sam. Sam reached for a tin can supplied by boB.

Sam twisted the key attached to the can off of its side. boB glared at him in obvious disapproval. Sam looked at him innocently.

"If everyone has grabbed a can, I'll lead us in grace," boB said correctively to Sam through clenched and grinding teeth.

boB led and the rest followed as he said, "Hi. My name is Bob. I six year old. And I did not want a diary for Christmas. I want a rocketship."

"Good Times!" the rest bellowed.

Sam began unwinding his canned meal, his eyes avoiding contact with the others, his mouth concealing a smile of apparent bewilderment.

The black-haired woman stared across at him with sunken angry eyes. "Something funny?"

"No, I'd like a rocketship, too," Sam chuckled.

"Do our beliefs amuse you?" boB asked.

"A little." Sam smiled.

"We take our beliefs very seriously. We are living in the end times."

"I see. Are you saying you're afraid of judgment?" Sam asked.

"No. We have nothing to fear. Law is made to protect us. Judgment has apparently been poured out on the world. But I am fortunate to have found the book of our leader."

"And we are fortunate to have found you!" the black-haired girl said, her eyes fluttering even harder than before.

"Good Times!" the others chanted, picking up their cue without missing a beat.

"Then I'll definitely want to check this journal out for myself," Sam said sincerely.

"I think that's a good idea," boB said, taking a bite out of his dinner. "The sooner you two become acquainted with our leader's rules, the better."

Sellia turned to make conversation with other converts at the conference table rather than brave her potted meat.

"What's your name?" Sellia asked the scrawny teen.

"I'm Rab!" he said excitedly. He rocked in place and fidgeted with his blonde hair, brushing it out of his leering eyes. Sellia tried to focus on those black pupils, but as she did they would crawl across the walls, up on the ceiling, and down the front of her dress.

"Well that's original," Sellia said.

"It's my new name."

"Named for ... your leader?"

"Our provider, yes."

"Well my name is Sell—"

"No, we only name ourselves in ways that honor our leader," boB corrected.

"Oh, I didn't know," Sellia said.

"Yes," Rab said, "that's Berty, and that's Bobacita," he continued, pointing to the old woman and the black-haired girl, respectively.

"It's rude to point," Bobacita said, apparently bored with her meal, poking its sponge-like texture with her index finger.

"It's not in the book, so I don't have to follow it," Rab asserted.

"But it offends me; that *has* to matter to you!" Bobacita yelled.

"Quiet! We are one family; we do not oppose each other. We are not Wallace," boB pronounced. With boB's warning, the two were instantly quiet, the loud silence almost tangible. For a moment, Sellia even considered eating in order to excuse herself from the quiet.

"Can I see the book now?" Sam asked.

Bobert slid the leather journal across the table to Sam with a tired, laden movement. Bobert stared down at his cold meal in dissatisfaction while Sam immediately flipped the book open and began reading.

"So now someone's reading at the table. That's OK?" Bobacita asked.

"As long as it's not the Chauncey Pepper series," Bobert said in weary disgust.

Bobacita let out an aggravated sigh.

"I'm going to take a nap...for guidance," boB said, getting up from the conference table. He looked to Sam. "That's in the book, too. Somewhere in the middle."

"Are you really going to read that?" Sellia whispered softly in Sam's ear.

"I just want to know what we're dealing with here."

"Maybe a hint on how to get to the West Side?" Sellia asked.

"That's forbidden," Bobert said.

"Only by the fire-men," Rab said.

"But boB doesn't approve," Bobacita said.

"I don't see why anything about the West Side would be in here," Sam said. "This obviously predates the disaster. Why would there be information on how to get to the West Side?"

"The book has been known to offer guidance and even predict things that happen. As we emulate it, it emulates our lives," Bobert said. Sam nodded and went back to skimming the book.

"But the book doesn't forbid going to the West Side. No bad omens or anything?" Sellia asked.

"No," Bobert relented, "but there are better ways to survive listed in the book."

"Like what?" Sellia asked intently.

"I'm sure boB would rather share them with you himself," Bobert mused.

"So, when will we try these ways of survival? Or are we just going to stay here and die like boB said?" Sellia began, getting agitated, her voice cracking as it inflected.

"No, no," Bobert said, "that's not what he meant. He meant, if that is what is to become of us, then that is what will happen. We are dependent on the destiny the leader provides us with."

Sam giggled as he read the book. The Bobbers stared at him with contempt.

"And by leader you mean the, um...the B-man?" Sellia asked cautiously, fearing that sometime they would miss and spit on her.

"Yes, the provider!" Rab said.

"Rab, I've told you before, no one calls him that!" Bobert said.

Sellia pressed her inquiry, "So, when? When will these signs come?"

"When they come," Bobert said.

Sam stood and departed the room from the same exit boB used.

"I guess he doesn't have any faith," Rab said. "Are you going to eat that?"

Sellia looked up in astonishment before realizing he was talking to her. "Uh, no. Help yourself." She slid it to him before standing to leave, departing in a different direction from boB and Sam.

"Do you know your way around yet?" Berty asked.

"I'll be all right," Sellia said, defense tinting her voice.

"Best to stick close by till' you do," Berty said.

Sellia walked off alone. She almost ran through the cubicled hallways as fast as she could, just because she was told not to. But after reaching the next room she slid against one of the carpeted walls that coursed throughout the innards of the complex, static messing up the hairs of her head.

She remembered how lonely she was only a few hours ago, and how lost she was. Wherever she went she could only find more distraction. And Sam.

"Hey, am I interrupting anything?" Sam asked as he bounded into her room with his broad Cheshire smile dimpling his face.

Sellia once again attempted to avoid contact with Sam. She still detested him and his fedora, which was temporarily MIA. And she still could not convince herself why she bothered to save him. *It was because of the hat,* she insisted to herself. That and the gore she would have had to endure to be rid of him.

"So, I've been wondering," Sam started, "what was your past like? You're very beautiful. You must've had—"

"The next phrase out of your mouth had better be something trivial like 'nice shoes,'" Sellia jabbed.

"I hope you have a point to go with that blade," Sam parried. "I was going to say 'a good life.'"

"Beauty isn't any indication of that."

"You must've had money to keep yourself beautiful."

"Are you calling me old?"

"I mean you must've had someone."

"Why all the interest in me? I'm not the weird one sitting in the middle of nowhere singing and dancing in a dead world! Who are you?"

"Would you rather have found me crying? Maybe I can't find the people that matter to me. Or maybe I already have. And maybe I just found out I lost someone close to me. And the only way I can hold onto my last shred of sanity is to sing."

His voice trailed off just for a moment as Sellia began to grasp a larger picture, "Really? Is that what happened? I'm sorry. I might've come across..." she said sincerely.

"No. None of that happened. I lived alone. But you really should be more sensitive to a person's singing habits. It could lead to some pretty dark secrets sometimes," Sam said lackadaisically.

Sellia opened her mouth, preparing to object loudly to Sam and everything about him when Rab ran by.

"boB lost his sock!" he exclaimed before he ran on.

Sellia looked at Sam quizzically. Sam just smiled.

"You might want to—" Sellia started.

"I'm checking, I'm checking!" Sam said, still smiling, his nose in the book.

"I think he wants us to follow him," Sellia said.

Sam stood and walked out the door, reading a line with each step.

"I woke up this morning with one sock; either the bed ate it or I don't know, but, wow, was my day horrible. I had a customer yell at me. Leesa bought the shoes I put on hold for myself. Just to spite me, I'm sure. What use has she got for steel-toed galoshes? And as usual I came home with a pocketful of shoe filler paper and stockings. Good Times."

"OK, and this means—?" and Sam halted, Sellia bumping into the back of him, her chin briefly coming to rest on the top of his head with the backlash.

The Bobbers were in front of them, all gathering around boB. Sellia observed that he did, indeed, have on only one sock.

"My sock was taken from me as I napped. We must be on guard. We have no idea what may befall us today. I know what you're thinking. Some of you are thinking that our new friends here are the trouble. Well, I can assure you that's simply not the case," he said.

"Well, why not?" Bobacita asked.

"They *are* with us, aren't they? They follow us and seek our ends. Are we wrong? Are we now to second guess ourselves?" boB said.

There was a swell of no's and of-course-not's from the congregation.

"Those who are not with us are against Bob's will," he said. boB paused and waited for the congregation to finish their chorus of spits. "Those are cowards, too lazy to find us, too foolish to walk out their doors and down the street."

"Good Times!"

"Well, why are the new folks hiding behind everybody if they're with us?" ventured Rab.

Eyes looked toward Sellia and Sam.

"We're bringing up the back," Sam said.

"Good Times," Sellia agreed, pumping her fist in the air.

"That's my job," Berty said. As she did, she shoved Sam toward boB. Sam tugged Sellia with him.

"We must prepare for departure! It's not safe here anymore," boB said. Then, looking to Sellia, he asked, "Do you have any questions?"

"On a scale of one to ten, how culty do we have to be to stay?" Sam whispered in her ear.

Ignoring Sam, Sellia asked, "So, what is so special about the leader?"

"He spent his life giving people soles," boB said.

"Excuse me. Could you mean, selling shoes?" Sam asked.

"Shut up, you happy heretic," Sellia whispered over her shoulder.

"Do you two have something to discuss?" boB asked.

"No," said Sellia

"Yes," said Sam.

"How are we going to leave?" Sellia asked.

"We have a plan to accomplish that," boB said.

"Is this by any chance Bob's plan?" Sam asked.

The congregation spat. This time Sellia did, too.

In Heaven

The Fish Eater cackled in delight while Bob began wondering if it would be possible to vomit in heaven.

"You certainly have made yourself busy," The Shining Man said. "I'm surprised you're not focusing on your other problems. It's a big world down there, and you are only one."

"You can't save them all," The Fish Eater shot back. "Remember that. Remember that!" The Fish Eater flung his cloaks at Him and then stomped away. The Shining Man giggled and looked at Bob.

"Lord, why did You make me watch that?" Bob said.

"When I deliver Lucifer into your hands, Bob, I want you to understand what this has been about," The Shining Man said. "This is the first step of your victory."

THE JOURNAL OF BOB

Excerpt from June 16th: one month from previous entry

Did I mention that Wallace likes to talk? Not only does Wallace enjoy talking to customers and employees, turns out he talks about us, too.

Meredith and I have found a surprising amount of things in common. We have the same taste in movies and books, we're both only children...and neither of us is crazy about Wallace right now.

Turns out Wallace has been hitting on a lot of the female employees at Archers, and he made an enemy of Meredith. She wouldn't be specific, but I had heard him talk enough to know that he had found nasty innuendo in the act of trying a shoe on someone.

After weeks of suffering Wallace's burning stares during our conversations, Meredith and I found ourselves scheduled on separate days for this week...and next week. Several employees asked me about my "relationship" with her. Jon tipped me off that, ultimately, this has been Wallace's doing, too.

I was boiling mad today. Finally I had someone to open up to at the store and now was getting flack for it. When I came back from my lunch break with mustard on my shirt, I saw her reorganizing multi-colored bottles on the counter behind her. As I approached, she watched me in the mirror.

"Well, I just heard from Susan and Jake that we've been dating for two weeks," I said.

"Is that all? I heard it was two months," she said.

"That's crazy! We've only known each other a month."

"I know." She looked down and touched another bottle but did nothing with it but turn it clockwise in place.

"Say, would you like to go to dinner after work? Or would that be weird?"

"Not at all," she said, turning her head over her shoulder with a smile. "Lets!"

Good Times!

Chapter 6
CONVERT-SATION

"**S**O, WHAT IS THIS PLAN?" SAM ASKED. "WHAT ARE WE going to do?"

"If you read the book, you'll know what we're going to do," Rab retorted.

"Um, I am," Sam said.

Sellia walked toward boB as the others circled around Sam to evangelize him. "Tell me how you found out about, you know…"

His whisker be-speckled, thick cheeks peeled back to allow a smile. Though the smile was tilted, it seemed less mangled and demeaning than before. He waved her away from the group to a door in the back of the room. He opened the door to reveal a series of other doors through a sprawling corridor. Left, right, right, stairwell up a few floors, left, left. She gave up trying to trace her way back after the fifth turn.

Somewhere in the labyrinth of hallways and cubicles they stopped. They were in an open area filled with cubicles. In the middle of the room laid an overturned mail cart. A cave-in at the opposite end of the room had placed a large rafter through the right wall of cubicles. Sellia could see from where she stood that some had never left their desks. The green-gray room was alive with the stench.

"Oh! Oh, God!" Sellia was on her knees, dizzy from the smell. A vague faux instinct crossed her mind for a moment that maybe smell, like heat, rises to the ceiling, allowing fresh air to be on the floor. As she took in a breath near the floor, all she could do was mix the odor of mildewed carpet into the aroma.

"Do you know what happened?" boB asked.

"No one cleaned up this room?"

"Do you know how all of this got started? What happened to our city?" His eyes seemed frantic.

"I thought you knew. Didn't what's his name—"

"No, he never told me." He looked down dejectedly. "He never speaks to me."

"Then how'd you get that journal?"

"I got it here." The smell did not seem to bother him at all as he walked a few steps forward to the mail cart. "I used to push this around everyday. But then one day the lights flickered and died and the room shook. The very next thing I knew, I was on the floor, the cart was toppled, and that book was on the ground right in front of me. I don't consider myself superstitious. But I do believe in destiny. When I came to, I got up and immediately cracked my neck because, as you can imagine, it was stiff. My eyes casually glanced over the page. The first thing, the very first thing I read, was, 'When I got up this morning the first thing I did was crack my neck.'"

boB outstretched his hands, his eyes wide with anticipation, prodding her to respond.

"Sounds interesting," Sellia said.

"That's not all. Next, I scratched between my eyebrows with my ring finger and what do you think the blessed book said about that?"

"It said the same thing," Sellia said with no enthusiasm.

boB nodded with the sincerest approval. "It said the exact same thing. So for kicks, I decided to follow the next page and a half word-for-word as best as I could. I stretched my arms, like Bob, I yawned, as big and as loud as I could imagine Bob yawning. And then I started walking. He walked outside, so I walked outside. And the second that I started walking, the light fixture came right down from the ceiling here and smashed where I had been laying. He saved my life! There's the proof right at your feet."

"I'm sure it's just a coincidence."

"Can you afford that risk?" he grunted.

"So," Sellia looked down at the shattered fixture, wanting to change the subject to a less zealous one, "you've lived here the past few days?"

"Just long enough to get converts. You see, we don't have much time. We are going on a pilgrimage very soon to Bob's house. Everything we need will be there. And in his driveway is a boat. A boat that he has used to cross the river dozens of times. If we can make it to the boat, we'll be able to stay afloat when the flood comes. And now that we have the sign, we know it's time."

"Flood? Did the book tell you this?"

"There are themes of fish and water throughout the manuscript. It's evident. And with the rains this past week, it seems to be the most likely outcome. My first instinct was to return to my house, but it was already gone. It's only a matter of time before the whole city just sinks."

On the way back to the main hall, boB and Sellia could hear the low rumble of a church split breaking the tranquility of the office chambers. As they came closer they began to distinguish the voices.

"No! That has nothing to do with anything!" Berty insisted.

"Really?" Sam asked. "I would think apostolic succession would be important. None of you are endowed to be head boB after boB passes?"

"Well, I could. I mean, I relate to Bob," Rab said.

The congregation spat.

"How dare you compare yourself to our…Bob," Bobacita said.

The congregation spat again.

"Well, I'm sure it's in here," Bobert said. "It'll be in here and everything will be cool."

Sam handed him the book as he asked, "Can you also tell me if the book of Bob is synoptic or not, because that would really trouble my faith if I found out it wasn't."

By this time the congregation's unified throat was dry. The door creaked open in a ceremonial moan to the main hall as boB walked in, Sellia trotting behind him.

Rab ran up to boB. "If you should leave, who takes over?"

boB looked at Rab blankly, "Leave where?"

"Leave here."

"I mean *to* where?"

"Anywhere."

"I haven't chosen anyone."

"Well, didn't, you know, *he* choose anyone?"

"Not that I know of."

"Well how'd he choose you?"

"The book found me."

"But it didn't say that you should be the boB?"

"I, uh—who started you asking this?"

Sam stood in the middle of the congregation, smiling in devilish amusement.

boB marched in a beeline to Sam, "You?" He plucked him up by the arm and carried him out the same corridor to enlightenment that he had taken Sellia. boB marched faster this time and sometimes made Sam step in rapid succession in order to keep from being dragged.

Sellia saw boB haul Sam off and began to trail them out of pure curiosity, being careful not to make it too obvious. She dogged their movements and darted behind corners as they marched toward their destination.

When at last boB reached the room with the glass-covered floor, still pungent with death, he began, "It's time for you to tell me why you're here. What are you after? Do you want to be saved, or do you just want the girl?"

Sellia felt disembodied from her stomach. Suddenly without an organ to rest on, her heart sank to the bottom of her rib cage where it became entangled with her small intestine; even without the smell of decomposed flesh haunting the room, she would have felt the same. Completely, medically subdued by the thought of Sam's answer, her mouth dangled open in an act of kittenish horror.

"It seems to me you're acting a bit like Wallace," Sam said, as boB seemed more than a little uneasy, "finding ways to separate me from the girl," Sam observed. "I'm a quick study."

"Don't get over-spiritual on me! Don't be such a literalist," boB said, pumping out his words with vehemence.

"Well then, what gives you the right to claim you know how to save people? You write a book and capitalize on the already dashed dreams of people to give yourself power," Sam said.

"What right have you to judge me? To tell me what I've done and why I've done it? You're the arrogant one. You're a divisive character, and you belong separate from this community," boB fired back.

Sam smirked with approval. "I sure do," he smiled. He leaned up against the wall, grinning, his eyes fixed on boB in satisfaction of his excommunication.

boB turned his back on Sam and pushed through another door in the hallway.

Sellia walked up to Sam, sliding the glass away from her with the sides of her feet, "What on Earth was that about?"

"Nothing."

"Nothing? You were a complete jerk to that guy. Sure, he may be a little off, but at least he's trying. You're just being a problem. You're just wading. You're just treading water."

"And I can see he's got you thinking about the flood," Sam said as Sellia snapped her head back in response. Sam continued, "Yes, this whole city is going to flood. Most likely your West Side, too. I didn't want to talk about it earlier. I thought it might disturb you. But I didn't completely forget about the possibility of it. I knew if we stayed here much longer we'd get swallowed by it." Sam pulled a familiar object from his pocket and tossed it to Sellia. It landed on her shoulder.

"It's his sock," she said, shocked that such a disgusting object could be so pleasing to her.

"I just wanted to move things along," Sam said. "I wasn't completely sure what it would do, but I hoped it would get him moving. Looks like it worked. It scared him into action."

"I'll say," and Sellia grew despondent, "Guess that means there's no destiny, no providential coincidences. It was all engineered by you."

"Sheesh, you try and do something nice for someone, you save their lives, and then they're upset it wasn't divinely accomplished?

I'm done," Sam said walking away, his arms thrown in the air. "By the way, where are you going?"

"Bob apparently has a boat," she said.

"Good for him."

"I'm sure there's a way we can talk boB into letting you tag along. I think he'll listen to me."

Sam's brow stood on end. "Listen, huh? Well, I really don't even want to be here anymore, so I'll be seeing you, or not at all, as the case may be."

"You don't know the way out."

"I'll find one."

She grabbed his arm, "You can find one once you're back in the main hall." She led him back to the hall, firmly holding on to his sleeve the entire way. She almost made a wrong turn once or twice, but her instincts led her through the corridors. Once back in the hall, angry, glaring eyes from the congregation forced her to let go of Sam's sleeve.

She looked back at him as her feet carried her farther from the place where he was standing. boB, back from his sojourn from the other hallway, hovered near her to say, "I appreciate your neighborliness, but you should've left him up there to find his own way back."

"Maybe," she said. "So, I suppose you won't let him come along with us on our pilgrimage."

"He doesn't believe."

"You shouldn't give up on him."

"It's a choice. He made his."

"What if he just stayed in the back of our group? What if he never said anything?"

"Why does this matter to you? Why do you care?" boB asked, his menacing smirk twitching defensively.

Sellia looked around the room for a moment, thinking and inventing. "Because Bob told me to."

The room looked at her with pride, awe, admiration, and a contingent of jealousy. Sam, however, wanted to spit.

THE JOURNAL OF BOB

It is noted in a later entry that she had a salad while Bob had a chicken salad sandwich. This reflects the union of the two.

—BOBERT

Excerpt from June 16th: same entry

Dinner was a little awkward at first. In addition to still being dressed for work, we both realized that we had never been in any other setting with each other. Other than that, we picked up where we left off, conversing a little about everything.

(...)

She told me she wanted to leave the store. I told her I understood, but that I'd prefer it if she could stay at least a little while longer.

(...)

She stayed. And come to think of it, she didn't put up much of a fight.

Chapter 7

HEXCOMMUNICATION

IT WAS TEN O'CLOCK ACCORDING TO SOME LUMINESCENT dial that still managed to work. As that had been Bob's bedtime for more than a hundred pages, boB saw fit that everyone followed the example.

Sellia lay in the honored center of the congregation's huddle on the lump of clothes provided for her. She cuddled with herself beneath someone's oversized sweater. She watched Sam through the dim side-glow of a flashlight as she tried to become comfortable on her makeshift mat. He took up space in an empty corner as he folded a used dirty-blue shirt to be his pillow.

She turned around and saw boB. He lay on his left side. His stare was unshakable.

"Goodnight," boB said as he reached for the flashlight and turned it off.

When Sellia awoke it was by boB's subtle nudge. He handed her a glass jar filled with water.

"What is Tiffany's serving?" Sellia yawned as she woke up.

"What?" boB asked.

"Never mind," she sighed.

"Come on. We're leaving."

"Now?"

"Yes, now. If we wait any longer we'll risk losing Bob's house to the flood water." He took her hand, almost literally, for there was no resistance, and tried to stand her upright.

"Let go of me," she heaved. She looked for Sam and found him leaning next to the door holding his very own jar of water.

The rest of the congregation distanced themselves from him as they gathered around the scribe called Bobert.

"The house we seek is 3111 Celeste, and that means that we are compelled to follow Ayles and then Elm for eleven blocks until we arrive," Bobert said to the resounding reply of "Good Times."

Sam methodically took steps around the throng of Bobbers. "Funny how Bob actually wrote directions to his own house," Sam said. His eyes smiled.

"Yeah. It is," she smiled.

"Time to go," boB interrupted, tugging Sellia and pushing Sam with only his eyes.

The Bobbers were cluttered near the door, piled and cramped, though the lobby was spacious and accommodating. As Bobert opened the door, the converts spilled out onto the landscape.

Sellia squinted her eyes upon emerging from the cavernous tomb of the believers. The world, so drab and bleak hours earlier, was vivid now by comparison to the dull hall. The gray here was brighter than the gray of the cavern; the man-made ceiling had blotted out even the promise of the sun that hid behind the clouds.

The pilgrimage started out in a great huddle, but as time and landmarks passed the distance between each member became greater. The exodus now became a string of people, each separated by five steps.

Bobert led them, cradling the Book of Bob in his arms. boB followed a step behind, occasionally checking on Bobert to see if their course remained true, then Sellia, then Bobacita; Sam was holding up the end. As the distance between each Bobber grew, Sam shifted up a spot in line. Soon he came close enough to hear boB say this line:

"Bob told me I should marry you," he said to Sellia with complete conviction.

Bobacita spat in Sellia's direction.

"He didn't tell me that," she shot back. "And didn't you say that he never speaks to you?"

"Um, well, I inferred that uh, since we... I understand." boB sped up and began re-charting the course with Bobert.

"You handled that well," Sam peeked from fifth in line.

"I'm getting the hang of the place," Sellia said with a smile.

boB turned around to grimace at Sam for a moment before continuing to his work of finding the way. Encouraged, Sam shifted around Bobacita. "Let's get out of here," Sam said, a twinge of excitement ebbing his voice.

"Excuse me?" Sellia said.

"What can these bozos do for us? Let's get away, find another road. Or maybe we can go back to the studio. At least I had food there for both of us."

"And no can opener!" Sellia laughed. "No, Sam. You don't know where you're going, either. I mean, I could go with you. But if you and I went off together, we wouldn't be following anything more than ourselves. We were lost before. Maybe this isn't perfect, but at least we're trying."

boB turned back to smile and even wink at the unsuspecting Sam.

Sam bit his lip, "All right. We'll stay a bit longer."

Sellia looked down, feeling a little guilty for inadvertently giving a point to boB in the invisible tennis match he and Sam seemed to be engaging in.

"Food!" A shrill voice called out on the corner. "Do you have any provisions to spare?" a man shouted from atop a street corner. A building had crumbled and left this particular bum with a perch that contained parallels between the Mount of Olives and a mound of sackcloth and ash. The beggar crouched in place and reached toward the line of Bobbers, his frail hand interrupting a conversation between boB and Bobert as he asked again, "Do you have anything for me to eat?"

boB reared his head back in disgust. The old man had a kindly glint in his eye and a tilted broad-rimmed fishing hat on his spherical head. A dusty green trench coat cascaded from his hole-filled sweater, collecting at his feet. A beard wrapped its way around his face as stray teeth stuck out from his lips.

boB looked to Bobert and whispered, "Can we do that? What does it say?"

"The book doesn't mention giving anything to beggars," Bobert diagnosed.

"Sorry. We can't help you," boB delivered back to the beggar. By now Bobacita and Sam had caught up.

Bobacita repeated his reply. "We can't help you."

"Why not?" The bum tilted his head. To Sellia it didn't seem as much of a complaint as an intellectual challenge.

Bobacita turned her head to boB. boB simply shrugged and said, "It's out of our hands."

"Whose hands is my fate in?" the bum asked.

"His," boB answered, as Bobert supplied the text that revealed the leader's name.

"Bob?" the bum asked.

The congregation minus Sam and Sellia spat.

"Don't speak his name!" boB said. Sellia sat down, having seen this all before.

"What's the point of having a leader if you can't call on his name?" he bum asked. "How can he help you?"

"He left us this book," Bobert said as boB pondered the question.

"That's nice," the bum said.

"Do you want to hear of our leader?" boB asked.

"Not really," the beggar answered.

boB acted as though he had been slapped, even going as far as stepping back a couple of times. It seemed odd for Sellia to watch a big man put on such an obvious show. "Why not?" boB bellowed.

"Because if his followers won't help me, he won't watch over me."

"Well, that's just not true!" Bobacita insisted.

"Yeah! Bob cares!" Rab yelled back. The Bobbers spat.

"Where is he? Have you met him?"

Sam leaned over to Sellia. "I love this guy!" he said.

boB's pale face now inflamed, he raised his voice, "Who are you to challenge Bob?"

"Me?" the beggar asked. "Well...I'm God."

The Bobbers plunged into outrage as Sellia cocked an eyebrow.

Sam looked at her with a grinning expression that asked, Why not?

"What makes you God?" boB asked angrily.

"Well, didn't God Himself say that whoever did unto the very least of these does it unto Me? Well, look at me. Not a home. No food. Not a possession to my name. I am the least of these. God likens Himself to me, and that likens me to Him."

"I think we go north from here," Bobert interrupted.

"Do we?" boB said excitedly, glad to get away from the most confusing confrontation of his career as a prophet. The two of them took off and the rest of the Bobbers followed closely behind.

Sam and Sellia stayed behind. Sam shook his head, smiling as the Bobbers passed him and ladled judgment upon the three of them with their eyes.

"Well, you know what? If you were God, you'd be my kind of fellow," Sam said with admiration.

"'Cause I made him angry?" the beggar asked. "Don't you think I can make you angry?"

"Huh? Why would you do that?" Sam asked.

"Because the world is ending. It's taking sides, and you're just along for the ride." The beggar's voice was warm, not sardonic or condescending.

Sam smiled at him again. Sam shook his head as he strolled after the Bobbers, forty paces behind.

It was Sellia's turn to talk to the beggar. She was afraid of this oracle, afraid that he would take one look at her and tell her that she was a materialistic heathen. Of course, with the bracelets and necklaces still weighing her down and the gown that still had the price tag on it, a prophet or seer wasn't needed.

"The city is flooding," Sellia said. She said it with the tone connoting all the seriousness of a casual, "So, how was your weekend?"

"Only a matter of time," he smiled.

"We're going to find a boat if you want to come along," Sellia offered.

"I've already found a way. Thanks, though," the beggar said.

He rose from his seat, ash rolling away from the vanishing valley of his lap.

Sellia ran to catch up with Sam. As she joined him, Sam took a glance over his shoulder at the departing bum.

"I like him, you know," Sam said to her.

"I know."

After that, Ayles finally begot Elm, and the pilgrims seemed thankful for the change in scenery. Elm did not offer as many tall buildings, opting instead to showcase more humble shops and pawn brokers. It was easier for Sellia to digest the decadence of these ruins; in fact, some looked unchanged either because nothing had happened to them or because they had always been beyond repair.

Berty looked back at Sam and Sellia, only to shake her head in reply to something only she was thinking. Sam caught her glance and waved.

"So, why do you like him? I mean, you don't like boB," Sellia said after a minute of mulling the question over.

Sam sighed. "Good point, but I guess it was because he didn't... well, he had authority, I guess. I can't put my finger on it. But he didn't make me feel half as dirty as boB has. Even though, remarkably, they're saying nearly the same thing."

"Are you ever going to choose sides?"

"When the 'good guys' show up, I will. How about you? You taking sides yet?"

"I don't even know who the teams are," Sellia said

Sam laughed, then tried to stifle himself. "You and I, I would call seekers. We have searched, but we haven't found yet." His tone was sing-song.

"Maybe searching is enough?"

"Is searching enough for you? Can searching be enough when other searchers keep throwing us off the trail?" Sam gestured toward the Bobbers.

Sellia was quiet, churning Sam's statement over in her mind, when her thought process was interrupted by a shout from Bobert.

"Lunch time!" he yelled. "Lunch break was always at twelve ten. It is twelve eleven now. We resume our trek in thirty minutes!" Bobert then began passing out sandwiches to the rest of the Bobbers. When he came to Sam and Sellia, he handed her a sandwich and begrudgingly thrust one to Sam.

"It was hard to find. Low provisions and all," Bobert said as he turned away.

Sam flipped the lid of his sandwich to see a thin slice of ham, "Was it hard to make, too?"

Sellia found herself laughing at Sam's joke. They reached a curb and sat together as the others huddled a few yards away.

"Now, I gotta know something," Sam said. "A day ago I could barely keep a conversation going without you running away from me. Why are you now…gosh, it sounds like I'm complaining, doesn't it? I'm not! I'm definitely not!"

Sellia just smiled as she focused on her sandwich.

"Now, that's not fair," he smirked. "You need to answer me at least one question. How about this: why'd you save me from that monster? You just couldn't stand the sight of blood again?"

"Close," she said through a mouthful of ham. She showed him the back of her hand as she attempted to cover her mouth. "It was your hat."

"Excuse me?"

"Your hat's your trademark. Or at least that's what I thought. To me it was. You can't die without your hat." Her hand still covered her face like a bride's veil or a mystery mastermind villain on the late-late show. He took her hand, guiding it down with his fingers. Sellia clicked.

"Are you two…together?" It was boB standing with a cocked fist on his left hip as he half-smiled, half-chewed his lip. The way he said *together* made Sellia aware it was a three-syllable word.

"Kinda early to slap a title," Sam started.

"Because if you are, you're going to have to follow our rules."

"Well, we're not! And if you're going to—" Sam was silenced when Sellia's fingers rested on his lips.

Her eyes locked on Sam's in adoration. "Tell me your rules, boB. Tell me them now."

boB stuttered for a second, apparently not expecting Sellia to be so willing or so amorous. But he never knew Sellia as the young girl on Drewery lane: the queen of the skating rink, the actress of the abundant show, on every boy's arm but still independently alone. In her house in the crow's nest of her loft, she was above all things—even the things that defined her: passion lipstick, backless dresses, the crinkling of money, theater popcorn, the tissue paper of empty shopping bags, the color yellow.

Not even Sam was familiar with her. Not like the concierge at the Alamo Lounge, or the sweet boy from across the street, or the dandy of Camelot Avenue. Sam would become all of them to her and perhaps already was as she stared at him with her wooden china doll eyes.

Finally finding words, boB spoke, "They're not easy rules. They're meant to test love. To see if it's true. Bob," he whispered the name this time, "created these rules to test his own relationships. He doesn't expect us to do anything that he hasn't already gone through."

Sellia snapped her fingers, "C'mon! Get with it, boB. I don't have all day."

boB smiled. "You do have all day. You have weeks in fact. There's a very strict no touching rule until the second date. And a no-hand-holding policy until the fourth."

"What are your rules on excommunication?" Sam asked.

"Pretty lenient so far," Bobacita said resentfully.

"I'm not asking for any favors here," Sam smiled in reply.

"So this first date...Any way we could start now?" Sellia asked.

"Absolutely. But we can't afford you to be un-chaperoned. Rab! Here!" To boB's decree, scrawny, seventeen-year-old Rab came running. His blonde hair flopped across his brow as he ran toward them.

"Rab, I need you to watch these two lovebirds," boB said as

he walked away. "You know, save them from their own amorous advances."

Obediently, Rab sat a few paces away. He had one knee pressed up against his chin as his back arched his bony frame in such a way that he appeared as a vulture.

Ignoring the feeling of religious voyeurism creeping upon them, they continued their conversation.

"So, what was it you first noticed about me?" Sellia asked.

"The way you kicked," Sam said.

"I'm sorry?"

"No, not at all, that's how I pick all my girlfriends. Sheer leg strength. That's the way I like them."

"I like your bracelet," Rab said.

Sellia ignored Sam's joke. "Which one?"

"All of them," he leered.

She laughed and tossed her muddy hair like she was on a California beach.

"They're making your arm green," Sam said, gnawing his sandwich.

"What?" She looked at him scornfully.

"From your 'bath' yesterday. The water tarnished them. When you remove them you'll see," Sam said.

"You never mentioned it before," Sellia said

"I never cared about the bracelet," Sam said.

"I do. It's one of the few things that I have that reminds me of—"

"Of what, being a spoiled debutante?" Sam asked, laughing it off as a joke.

"I should've left you on that bench." Sellia got up and marched back to the others.

The Bobbers got up as if they had been waiting for the movie to end and the credits to roll. Sellia looked at boB and witnessed him wink at Sam again, snapping his fingers into the shape of a firing gun.

Her rage died as she looked back to the scoreboard. boB: 30, Sam: love.

THE JOURNAL OF BOB

Excerpt from July 18th: one month from previous entry

Today, as I arrived at the store, Jon told me that Meredith had quit the night before. She had been scheduled to work today so instead when I found myself gazing to the perfume boutique I saw Ms. Couch, still seventy-five and looking every inch of it.

The day passed quickly as I tried to keep my head above water in my department. Every once in a while, I'd stop to pick up the trash that filled the endcaps and cluttered the aisles.

It continued much the same way until about four o'clock that afternoon. That was when she appeared, walking into my war zone like a spy, wary of being spotted by Wallace or maybe even Ms. Couch. But more than that, amidst all the paper on the floor and even without ribbons in her hair, she looked like an unwrapped present. She wanted to talk, but I couldn't get out of my mind the seemingly crumbling and gutted backdrop of my department as my eyes glanced over her head. I told her to meet me when I got off at eight o'clock.

I couldn't get away until eight-twenty. But still she waited. Each glance out into the white glaze of the mall made me all the more stir crazy to clock out.

We ended up talking in the parking lot for a long time after that, just saying good-bye, I guess. I finally admitted that I had to run to pick up tickets for Melvin and me if we wanted to see Red Ruse Run Friday at The Palisade like he and I had planned. I hugged her good-bye and watched her walk away.

(...)

I missed her already.

Chapter 8

SCHISM

IT TURNED OUT THAT BOB NEVER MENTIONED that he had chosen a house that was downhill. This was not a big deal unless one was backing into the driveway or if the entire city was flooding.

Which, of course, it was.

Water had already seeped down the hill and filled the basin full of murky brown soup. The inclined curb became beach, as it seemed that it started the sea that stretched back toward the city. Only the roof of Bob's house peeked through the still waters. Bob's boat floated peacefully a few yards from the house. It was red and white. Despite the collection of dirt and grime, apparent even from the shore, it seemed to have survived the destruction.

boB laughed. It was now that Sellia noticed the difference between his laugh and Sam's. boB restrained his laugh, almost to the point of it being a menacing cough. Sam was wild abandon while boB was force. Sellia shivered.

Noticing her, boB said, "It'll be warmer once we get to the boat." He smiled his cocky half smile like a man who had what he wanted and was winning. "Rab! Get the boat!"

Once again Rab obediently did as his lord ordered, jumping off the curb and swimming toward the abandoned boat. His frail body was tossed by the thin waves, but when he reached the boat and hoisted himself to the deck, he waved to the jubilant throng of Bobbers.

"Bring it here!" boB yelled.

"There's no key."

"What?"

"There's no key!"

"I heard you!" boB turned to the crowd in rage. "Bobert! Bobert! What does the book say? Where is the key?"

Bobert found the page that detailed one of Bob's fishing trips in his Bowmaster 2000, and told of the six-inch bluegill that was a source of much pride. Founder and scribe reread the passages detailing how Bob had one day lost his keys and scoured between couch cushions and piles of laundry before finding them in the pair of jeans he had worn the day before. After that, Bob "consecrated" a special place for his keys so that he would never lose them again.

Bobert's hand pointed to a distinct passage. In unison the two collaborators looked into the mouth of the basin: their final destination.

"It's in there," Bobert pointed to the cesspool sea surrounding the house's soggy black peaks. "Bedroom. Dresser. Top left," Bobert said with an air of finality in his voice.

"I'll do it," Sam said. "Break in the top, swim down, grab it, swim up."

boB gnashed his smirk. "Are you sure you even believe in our book?"

"Of course not, but if it gets us out of harm's way, it's a good deal," Sam said.

"The chances of survival are small," Bobert said. "If it's completely flooded, you'll drown before you even reach it."

Sam turned to boB, "Looks like you're running out of good reasons not to let me go." Sam started for the curb without waiting for a reply. Sellia peered out to the house to see the single, cycloptic window to the attic glaring back at her.

Splash!

Sam was in the water and already making progress toward Bob's house. Sellia crept up to the edge of the curb. The others watched her as if their eyes could somehow pull her back.

Plunk! Plink…plink…plunk. Sellia pushed the bracelets off her arms and watched them as they spun arcs into the black pool. She slipped out of her brand new shoes and left them on the curb. Before she jumped, she glanced at her arms. They were green.

Ploosh!

The water was freezing, and yet thick like tar. The slow paddle would have been impossible with the weight of the bracelets around her arms and wrists. Not wanting to taste the ingredients of the mystery water, Sellia kept her head above and safe, except for the occasional squirt across her cheek. Sam's hand was waiting and extended as she reached the roof.

"Nice swim," Sam said.

"They're playing us against each other," Sellia said, out of breath, her eyes wild and jittery as they bounced around her irises.

Sam laughed, dirty water running off his nose, "Of course they—"

Sellia interrupted him with a kiss, their relationship now keeping pace with the frolicsome gallop of her original lifestyle.

Ker-splot!

boB and Bobert leaped into the water and were now fighting to get to Bob's house before Sam and Sellia exchanged any more pleasantries.

"I'm going in, too!" boB shouted.

"Why you? We need you!" Bobert said.

"Who knows Bob's house better than me?"

Bobert attempted to spit out of the corner of his mouth while still treading water, but only succeeded in getting a mouthful of sea and deluge.

Once at the roof boB hoisted himself up with his muscular arms and stared down at Sam.

"Come along, brother. Maybe this pilgrimage will make a convert of you yet," boB said.

Bobert lifted up the window to the attic, never questioning why the holy threshold to his leader's home was filled with flaked white paint and tiny dead beetles. boB started and then motioned for Sam to go first. He did, and then boB, and then Sellia, and then finally Bobert followed. Bobert took a flashlight out of his belt, turned it on and then thumped it on the back for good measure. He handed it to boB.

"Top left, bedroom dresser," Bobert reminded.

"I got it, I got it," boB chanted.

Bobert looked at Sam. "It's only one story. Just go down the attic steps, into the hall, past the living room, and into the bedroom on the right at the end."

"Simple," Sam nodded.

"Unless it's flooded," Bobert nodded. "Bob thinks you guys are cool."

"You too." boB smiled his benediction to Bobert.

boB opened the trapdoor and began his decent into his lord's den. They both sank in the water, chest deep for boB and neck deep for Sam. The water knocked against Sellia's ankles as she watched from the steps while her two men trekked to rescue the icon from its chamber. They turned right at the end of the hall. Sellia watched the two of them disappear into the blackness with nothing but creaks and ripples to track them.

But she could hear them. Hear them as they talked about her. She leaned out over the water. She placed her right palm against the opposing wall, trying hard not slip against the slick condensation that dripped down the sides.

"Bobi, come back. It's not safe," Bobert said.

"Bobi?" Sellia said.

"It's your new name. boB said that—" Bobert started.

"Shhhhhh!" Sellia interrupted. "I can't listen with you talking."

The first voice she heard was the gravely and slow timber of boB's voice. "Want to…group has…abide rules…Sellia…limits."

Sam's voice snapped back quick enough to show anger but yet still be playful, still Sam-like. "No right…authority…dictate what is right and wro—"

Rummaging could be heard now.

No more voices. Only loud, violent sloshing.

One item floated down the hallway. With each slosh it traveled closer to Sellia. The item was small and ordinarily she wouldn't have seen it if it hadn't been for its neon coloring. Rearranging herself on the steps, Sellia reached out and caught it. There was a flotation device attached to a key chain.

Sellia began laughing, "It's a bobber. The key…is attached to a bobber."

Bobert jumped, "The key! You have it?"

Sam's voice came shining through. "Self righteous…thug…can't know…love is."

As she handed the key to Bobert to check the inscription she heard boB say, "Play by…own rules…cheerful bum."

"…no rules…grab…power…any reason," Sam said.

Sellia's mouth opened. The water now started to tremble and slosh even more than before.

"This is it!" Bobert yelled. "Bowmaster! I'll go get it started. You wait for them." Bobert ran up the steps.

boB's voice was clear this time. "If you really want to die for Bob…"

Sellia's jaw dipped lower as she saw even more ripples forming from the mouth of the distant doorway. She expected at any moment to see the color of blood emerging in the embers of light that shone now and then on the water.

Loud splashes and swimming came out of the bedroom on the right. A light flashed and burned Sellia's eyes in the darkness.

"Fool…you…I will…Where…ing to? Your…now!" It was boB, wading toward them with Sam swimming out in front. boB was yelling louder than she had ever heard him speak. *Sam has some talent,* she thought, not feeling that bad anymore about being occasionally angered by him.

But there were more ripples. Bigger and faster than those that had come before. The hallway shook. Teeth arose and decorated the walls. The white in boB's eyes caught Sellia's as the mouth closed on him. The narrow jaw snapped across the prophet like scissors. One gash, then two more. boB's flashlight hit the water as the hallway convulsed.

Sam reached the steps. "Go! Go!" He began pushing Sellia, fighting her default instinct that clicked in her mind whenever she saw blood. Holding her hand all the way, Sam helped Sellia through the beetle-filled window.

The boat was coming for them across the lagoon.

"Where's boB?" Rab called out.

The house was starting to shake visibly from the outside.

"Dead. The fish got him," Sellia said.

"What!" Bobacita screamed.

"What fish?" Rab retorted, becoming very teenagery.

Sam shook his head, insisting, "It's a monster. It eats people! You think that house is shaking on its own?"

"You don't get on without boB," Rab said.

"boB is dead. It killed him! I didn't!" Sam said.

"He's right! I saw it. Sam wouldn't stand a chance against boB. He'd get creamed!" Sellia said.

"Thanks, honey," Sam said more sincerely than he would've had their lives not depended on that fact.

"She is *your* girlfriend. And she is a brat. She'd say anything to save herself," Rab said.

"I got the key!" Sam said. "I saved your lives."

"I guess that might be why Berty hasn't shot you yet," Rab said just as Sam noticed the old woman pointing a rifle in his face.

"Keep smiling, pretty boy," Berty said, her finger not twitching, her eyes locked in a cynical and unwavering formation. "Keep smiling."

All Sam could manage was a grimace as he watched the water churn as the Bobbers left on another pilgrimage.

Sellia placed her hand against the roof as she leaned against it for a perplexed moment. She could feel the tremors vibrate through her palm as the house still shook.

"Let's make it to that curb as fast as we can while Moses is still inside." The two dove in the water and swam away from all they had followed for a day and a half.

THE JOURNAL OF BOB

Excerpt from July 18th: same entry

> I walked up to The Grand Palisade Theatre, its bright flashing neon lights made me even more depressed. Almost as if the bold letters on the marquee were broadcasting my inner humiliation. I began carefully dodging the people exiting from the six-thirty showing. I missed her. And I knew I'd carry that feeling for a long time.
>
> Then, in the next moment, the feeling was gone. Meredith was sitting on the bench in the midst of them, her hands folded and her platinum hair changing colors with the flashing lights. Was she waiting for me? Dazed and dizzy from the lights, I sat on the bench with her. I sat without saying anything for moments. We just stared off into the distance.
>
> Finally I took her hand and I kissed her, the noise of the crowd a hum, the neon lights a blur.

* * * *

The kiss itself is not a literal kiss, for we feel that would be a contradiction of boB's early "dates must be chaperoned" teachings, but rather this is a metaphorical representation of cleansing the inequity from the Meredith character, who was obviously backsliding in leaving Bob's store rather than staying for the final confrontation with Wallace.

—BOBERT

Chapter 9

TWILIGHT IN APOCALYPSE

THEIR FOOTSTEPS ECHOED OFF OF THE EMPTY houses as Sam and Sellia walked down Bob's road. They had no destination now, and without a word they had both agreed to wander to the end of the street, where a forest leaned.

"I almost miss them," Sam said.

"Why? You hated them. You disagreed with everything they said. This was what you wanted."

"Yeah, but not exactly the way I wanted it. I kinda wanted it to be my idea. Now I just feel rejected."

Sellia laughed. "We're better off traveling by land. This way we can stay away from Moses, and the Bobbers won't have you walking the plank." She placed her head on his shoulder and gazed at him with her eyes, those hungry opals that swallowed him with every glance and the eyelashes that batted coded symphonies to him.

They strolled along together, taking glances at the houses as they passed by. All seemed relatively intact. Some loose gutters, some window stripping missing. The item that stood out, the thing that was the most unsettling, was the mud. Brown, black, or grey, the sludge caked itself on the backside of each house, pointing toward the forest ahead of them. Caught up in the strange sight, Sam walked backwards to appreciate it.

"You're going to fall," Sellia said.

"I bet it was a blast to be a kid around here."

"What makes you say that?"

"That's the fifth tree house we've seen on this street," Sam said pointing to some obscure branch.

"I bet you've always been the same. I bet you were the same, devilish kid back in the third grade that you are now."

"I was impish," Sam said. He knelt for a moment to pick a daffodil from one of the abandoned lawns. He pinned the yellow flower in between locks of her dingy hair.

As he did so, Sellia could still smell the lingering whiff of Sam's cologne, and for the first time, she could begin to appreciate it. She diagnosed it as a blend of iodine and her own flask of Taboo No. 5.

"So, you got your first kiss wearing that musk? What was her name?" Sellia teased.

"Bianca," Sam said, turning again to walk backward.

"That was not her name!" Sellia hit him in his arm, again disgusted with him, if only slightly.

Sam shrugged. He looked past the trees and houses toward the sky. The gray clouds still hung about the firmament like old drapes.

"It's almost nightfall," Sam said, still walking toward the forest at the end of the road. The trees leaned in toward the cul-de-sac, heavy from the mud that clung to each of the needles. Each needle of the pines was black and twice the usual size. Overflowing water trickled down the hill. There would be no walking down it.

"Well, lets go back. Perhaps there's a house with a door I can jimmy."

"Back, Sam? Back?" Sellia laughed. She crossed her feet with each step in her languid sashay towards him. "Are you going to let a steep little hill stop you?" She had switched from cold to hot again.

Sam didn't seem to care as he stepped toward her advances. "I was just thinking of you. I know how you hate to get dirty."

Sellia smiled and gestured to her blackish-grey dress that failed to retain even a tint of yellow anymore. "Not gonna be a big loss here, Sammy." She tugged his collar along as she started walking backward towards the incline.

She slipped as her foot touched the mud and the earth gave way from under her. Sam lunged forward to stop her from falling and stepped into the muck himself. The two of them spiraled down the side of the slope, sliding, twirling, and tumbling until they were intertwined at the bottom—too dizzy to be able to untangle themselves.

Sellia had a drunken look about her, a cascading smile and vacant eyes. But however loopy she was, the more alert Sam became. His eyes tightened and concentrated, drinking in her visage. And in being more sober, it was he who untangled them.

At the foot of the hill there were dunes. For miles it seemed as if that was all there was. Mounds of white ash. A warm snow. The flakes still fell around them from the black sky. If one could just forget all the carnage of the backdrop, the skyline filled with broken edifices, gutted streets split in two, one might just find a wonderland.

Sellia planted her damp, bare feet and began wiggling her toes in the faux snow. She giggled as the gray flakes of ash fell around her and played their way through her hair. She licked the air, even while drying her tongue, in an attempt to taste the snow.

"Um, you don't want to do that," Sam said with a worried look, trying to put his hands on her shoulders.

But this was her wonderland, and so she continued playing with her true love, tossing ash in the air over her head, throwing herself into the dunes, spreading her arms and legs to make angels in the debris.

Sam took a step back into himself and turned away from her to engage in the sights. In this sea of dunes lay the centerpiece: a large metal canister. The remains of a bomb? A shell casing to the world's largest bullet? It was scarred and chafed with black soot. Its edges were frayed and bent back upon themselves like melted leaves.

He took several steps toward the giant tombstone before being stopped by Sellia.

"What do you think of me?" she asked. Combined with the white ash that now peppered her platinum hair, Sellia's usual radiance had an even more angelic appearance. Thinking of the question's answer blurred his eyes—even to the extent of giving Sellia a cloudy halo. The question was not so much a question in tone as a pronouncement. But Sam took it as one anyway.

He remembered that when he first saw her she was accompanied by a jazz ensemble performing the greats of every era with a riff he could still hear in his head. When he swayed in the town as she trotted off to the theatre, he imagined how it would be to…dance with her. She was a style, a masterstroke of beauty in a monochrome world. *His* monochrome world.

"Sam, I'm waiting," she reminded.

He was still remembering the tune, solid and brim with emotion. The backbeats pounding, still staying steady within his mind. The old lyrics grew cold, stale, and meaningless. On the spot and looking into her, he rewrote them:

> The world is ending
> But it's just a beginning
> And though there's death and cinder all around
> It can't compare with this love I've found.

Sam did a little jig in place, jumping, spinning, and acting out every musical fantasy on a pallet of white. Best of all, he wasn't even to the chorus yet:

> For it's twilight in Apocalypse
> And I've never seen two fuller lips
> Can our love be opportune
> As it's claimed by this eternal tomb?

Sellia was amused—but that was all. "Sam, I—"

Sam stepped up to her and sang very, very softly in her ear, changing from big-band grandstanding to coffee shop intimacy:

> You have no past; I have no future.
> A ghost and a corpse can make a nice couple.
> A love to nurture
> In the dust and rubble
> For it's twilight in Apocalypse…

He may have come up with even more, had he not been interrupted by Sellia, who kissed him in such a way that made the intimacy of the act look the same as if she was shouting across a crowded room.

She closed in on him. Kissing, breathing, kissing, as if there was something vital she was accomplishing in the repetition.

Eventually the kisses grew infrequent and she stopped. Thoughts had impounded her brain, and she was now top-heavy from their presence. She fell onto her back as her own thoughts overwhelmed her. She seemed her most content in this moment. No longer could she be mistaken for a drunkard. Her intense and pensive smile continued as her eager eyes watched as thoughts poured from the heavens like a meteor shower.

Sam draped his arm around her; she mistook it for the breeze. Had she looked his way she may have even been surprised that he was still there. The two nestled into the crevice of one of the dunes and watched the sun that no one saw set behind the sky and fill the world with a soft indigo night.

THE JOURNAL OF BOB

People are drawn to Bob, but he is misunderstood and they often end up going their own ways.

—BOBERT

Excerpt from July 20th: two days after previous entry

I was waiting for Melvin at The Palisade when a girl spoke to me. She was quite pretty, blonde, sweet face. She was wearing a yellow dress.

She walked up to me and looked me in my face quite bored and asked, "Are you waiting for me?"

"Um, no," then I smiled, "Not unless your name is Melvin."

"Ugh," she said rolling her eyes. Then she spun on her toes just like a ballerina in a music box and walked the other way.

Chapter 10

CREAM-COATED SAVIOR

SELLIA LAY IN THE NIGHT UNDER BOTH SAM'S ARM and her attentive thoughts, which now drifted over top of her. The string of nostalgia—days at the mall and gifts from forgotten beaus—so slow before, quickened its pace now as it tightened and became tangible. It first manifest itself as a voice that came in mannish window dressing.

It spoke and said nothing. No words. But Sellia cooed to the tenderness of its sound. These thoughts of self and its disembodied voice cupped their tendrils and dipped into Sellia's well. They drew out what she loved: square chins, trimmed hair, coupled biceps, six feet tall and with a niche for her head to rest on the sternum. Then the team of thoughts and disembodied voice created a husk from that blueprint and dressed him in yellow.

When Sellia opened her eyes, Bethesda stood before her.

"Good morning, love. Tiffany's is serving sterling silver necklaces and a side order of pancakes," Bethesda said.

Sellia yawned as she gazed at the yin to her yang, and then covered her mouth. She knew him. He had lived in her all these years. She sat up, wiping the dust from her hair for a moment. Then she looked at Sam, who had curled up next to her as he slept.

"Sellia, you've already said your good-byes. Don't tease yourself; I know you're not changing your mind," Bethesda said. His voice was sweet and unrelenting.

"I know," she got up in a fluid moment, bobbing down the dunes with care. "Which way are we headed?"

"West, remember? West Side Bridge," Bethesda smiled.

"Oh, yes," she reflected his smile. They turned northwest

simultaneously and began their trek in synch with one another. "This way, right?"

"You are right. It is that way."

"What do you suppose we'll find when we get there?"

"Windows with lights that shine like eternal furnaces, with halos that can be seen for eleven miles in every direction."

Sellia lifted her head and squinted all around her. The horizon was black without even the distant haze of lights. "I don't see anything." Sellia looked down to the ash. In disappointment she kicked it, sending a cloud billowing ahead of them.

"But you can see it," he corrected.

Out of the blackness she saw glowing haze and night separating like the rainbowed ripples of grease. It had always been there; even if it hadn't, she knew it had to be out there in the distance pulsing like a beacon: a dim pillar of fire.

Sellia's steps were cautious in the caked ash. In their repetitious duck-like motions, her bare feet ached and became sore. Bethesda massaged them as she walked, breaking his back to slither beneath her. She giggled as he twisted around her ankles and through her toes, only to restructure himself to join her again as her companion.

Handsome, translucent, and man-like in his countenance, he was there in all of the right ways, filling in the cracks left by Sam and boB. He was perfect in all the ways no real person could be. He was understanding of her in no way any god or spiritual leader ever would be.

"It's a much richer world over the bridge. No quarantine or bandits will keep us away." He was advocate for only one. "You were patient with Sam for long enough. He got you kicked out of that cult of suburban survivors."

"I'm not sure if that's a strike against him or an advantage," Sellia said.

"You even defended him just now. What a saint you are!"

"I suppose."

"You're my queen," Bethesda said, prideful of his prize.

She blushed and curtseyed before its invisible countenance.

They were passing through the forest now, the reflective pine needles, damp and slick with dew, were the only light in the muddy terrain. She slipped and fell. Attempting to get up, she fell again. Instantly, as she lifted her eyes she saw him at the top of the hill, cheering her on.

"You belong up here," Bethesda said, "Come on. Come!"

Sellia smirked with new courage and thrust her hands to the outstretched limbs of the pines. Her dusty fingers clutched the limp, rope-like branches and began pulling. Her feet skidded slightly into place as they worked their way up the hill. Like a jungle denizen, she reached for another limb to climb farther. She pulled and lunged with every new branch until she landed on her knees in the crackled gravel.

Bethesda smiled.

Sellia laughed as she picked herself up and began walking with him toward the city, backtracking along the path the Bobbers took.

"I should've never turned away," she said after a while. "I know I followed you in the beginning. But I began to feel guilty for doing that. I thought I was just following myself." Sellia shook her head in shame.

"So you followed others, believing that they knew better than you?"

"Yeah, I guess," she said sheepishly.

"Why do you doubt yourself? After all your years spent growing up and learning, you surrender to the man with the most demanding grip on authority. Ironically, those are the ones you should generally run away from."

"I see. It's obvious now. boB was a manipulator."

"And Sam?"

"Sam was just a really nice...boy," Sellia said.

They both laughed. They were facing each mud-caked house now. The sight, while ominous and foreboding before, seemed silly now as she walked with her invisible soldier.

"The important thing," Bethesda said, "is that you trust yourself."

"I suppose so."

"Who else is there? Sams and boBs only want to set you free according to their terms."

"Their terms?"

"Everyone believes what they want to believe. Their own slant on the truth. Everyone has one."

"But the truth—"

"Squat."

"What?"

"Squat on your knees. I want to show you something."

Sellia obeyed, squatting in the middle of the street, her joints cracking from the movement.

"Look ahead. What do you see?" Bethesda asked.

She noticed for the first time that the street sloped upward into a little hill in the middle, slicing her visibility in two.

"I see the houses here, the street, and the tops of the trees. Oh, and I see the light from the West Side."

Bethesda smiled at how she remembered their destination. "I see all of the houses. The trees, too. Not just their tops, but their trunks as well. Does that make what you see any less true?"

"No?" Sellia ventured.

"Exactly; we see two different ways." He squatted, too. "Now we see the same way. That's the benefit of having two sets of eyes. We have the potential to see it both ways."

Bethesda waited for a moment, letting his metaphors sink in as Sellia reveled at his wisdom and what it all meant. At last he said, "Let's keep going."

They began walking again. Sellia, confused, turned to him and said, "Give me another example."

"Love. Do you love Sam?"

This confused Sellia even more. She looked down to the dusty pavement. "What do you mean?"

Bethesda laughed.

"I suppose I did," Sellia said.

"You stuck up for him, you enjoyed his company, you maybe even believed in him. I'd say you did."

"OK, I loved him."

"Loved?"

"Love. I love him," she said, irritated.

"You also ran away from him. Three times. You're even running from him now. Do you love him, now?"

"No, I guess not. Are you going to tell me that I must not really love him and lay me up with a guilt trip?" Sellia asked.

"You're missing my point. Those statements, 'Yes, I do love him,' and, 'No, I don't love him,' are both true statements. Now how can that be?"

"Because...truth is—"

"Fluid. Truth is fluid. It changes. It fluctuates. Yours is different from mine, and mine from his, etc. Considering only points from column A, the answer is A, but while considering only points from column B, the answer is B. Combine them both and the answer is..."

"AB?"

"The answer is whatever column you choose to honor. Whatever person you find yourself being at the time. You see, you loved Sam this morning, but you were a different person then. Lets call her 'Sellia Alpha.' But considering these other facts, we can see that you don't love him now. So this is your truth, 'Sellia Beta.'"

"Sellia Beta," she smiled and giggled her little gleeful girlish giggle. She liked her new name. "This is why Bob's book is true for boB and the rest of the Bobbers and not for me or Sam?"

"Right! And?"

"Why it is right that I follow you and don't have to listen to everyone else's opinion."

"Good girl. Because you know the world is going to end. And that's why you want to go to the West Side. Where it's safer. Where you can make and follow your own rules."

"Right," Sellia said cautiously. She thought before that she only wanted to go because it was beautiful.

"As much as you'd like to play house with Sam, it's pointless when the house is falling down."

"Right," Sellia said confidently. *He's right*, she thought.

They walked for a minute more in satisfied silence. By now they were on Elm heading toward the glittering city.

"This place used to be beautiful," Sellia said at last.

"What do you mean, it used to be?" Bethesda said.

"Like I would have to tell you? Look over there. You can almost see the mall from here. The upper skylight is blown out."

"Yes, you know, you're right? The roof's crested with pristine, snowy ash. There's a warm breeze floating through. No traffic, the streets to ourselves. Whatever your heart desires—what a dump!" cackled Bethesda.

"I guess I should be happy," Sellia said sheepishly.

"You should be rejoicing."

"Sorry."

"What do you have to be sorry for? You are monarch of the West Side!"

Sellia looked around. Despite his reassurances, her kingdom still looked like a disaster area.

"Look, I will prove it to you," Bethesda said. He vanished. Sellia looked around frantically. Up, down, toward the roofs, toward the doorways. She began spinning in a desperate circle.

"Oh, my Queen!" Bethesda was a several dozen feet away smiling in an alleyway.

"How did you…?" Sellia said, bewildered, her nose twitching like a vexed rabbit. She walked after him, swinging her arms languidly.

"You need to be faster." Then *poof!* Bethesda was gone again. She ran to the spot where he stood mere seconds before. Her head twisted toward each direction that was conceivable for him to have fled to.

Laughter. To the right! Bethesda winked at her before he vanished again.

Sellia laughed, too, once she arrived at her next stopping point, cradled between mangled fire escapes and a billboard for Vargus and Vargus Personal Injury Law Firm.

Just a whistle. Left! This time he stayed in place. With each stride forward she thought that she might actually catch him.

Then he broke right and started to run. He would zigzag in his stride, trying to trick her into doing the same. Sellia burrowed through each alleyway, less graceful than she allowed herself to realize, pretending each clattering trashcan she toppled was another droplet of ashen snow.

Bethesda rounded a corner. As Sellia rounded the same corner she realized that she had lost him. *Forward,* she heard. *Keep going forward.* A clearing was ahead. She dove toward it with each passing stride. At last she arrived on the ashen, marble sidewalk. It was familiar. She looked around. Not as recognizable without the light pulsing from within, the bulbs that formed the neon lights wrote out the illegible pronouncement above the building: Grand Palisade Theatre.

"Where are you?" she teased. "Where are you?" she flirted.

"Here," Bethesda said. "You see? You're happier now. Don't you feel so much better? Doesn't this place look like a wonderland now?"

"I love you," Sellia blurted.

"I love you, too," Sam said. He was sitting on the bench behind her.

THE JOURNAL OF BOB

Excerpt from June 21st: one month prior to previous Entry

Today a man with a navy blue fedora walked into my department and sat down on a bench.

"Can I help you find anything, sir?" I asked.

"Just wanted to sit for a second. Long day."

"I hear that," I almost turned around and went back to cleaning a shelf.

But he said, "You wouldn't know the times for Red Ruse Run, would you? I gave myself the day off and decided I'd catch it."

"Yeah I'm guessing you'll want the two-fifteen showing."

"You must like it as much as me if you've memorized the times."

"Well, I guess I've been meaning to see it again. It's just so disjointed. The POV is inconsistent, and I think with all of its artistic camera shots it's just trying too hard. And there was so much subject matter I didn't agree with: the extended Dali-inspired drug trip, the philosophic theories they just kept bringing up..."

"Wouldn't blame 'em too much for the subject matter. They're just searching. When you think about it, searching is beautiful."

"Yeah, but it doesn't make for a good movie."

"At least they don't think they have all the answers," he said. "Searching is a destination of sorts."

"Really? Seems if you pack provisions for a

journey you plan to arrive at a specific destination. And if you don't..."
    "Then you die on the road," he finished.

* * * *

Huh?

—Bobert

Chapter 11

VARIATIONS ON A GOOD-BYE KISS

SAM HAD HIS USUAL SWAGGER ABOUT HIM AS HE rose, full of pomp, circumstance, and immaturity, but it seemed more pronounced and forceful as now his gait shortened and quickened with each step.

"I figured you'd be here," he said before looking to the ground to add, "just like last time. Are you talking to anyone in particular?"

"No," Sellia said innocently, turning her head west.

"Good, I'd hate to think that wasn't directed toward me."

"I...I don't love you, Sam."

"What, you don't *phileo* love me, or you don't *agape* love me? Cause it's pretty obvious you *eros* love me..."

"No, Sam, I don't love you in general. Oh, how'd he put this?"

"Who?" Sam asked.

"Don't argue with this one," Bethesda said. "He won't reason. He won't see. He is ignorance in its purest state."

"If you love me, just love me. It's a decision; just decide to," Sam said.

"That's your truth. You're entitled to it. But you must see that this is absolutely ridiculous. Would you look around? This world is over. It's o-ver. And you're talking to me like there's a future. That's why I left. I'm going to save myself. I'm going where the lights are. Across that bridge!" She pointed her finger violently behind her, oblivious that she was pointing in the wrong direction.

"And I thought you just wanted to go shopping again," Sam teased.

"No, that was a different me—Sellia Alpha. I'm Sellia Beta now."

"You come in models?"

"Ugh, you don't understand! You never change. You'll always

be the same little boy you always were. You'll never grow older or wiser or smarter or nicer or sweeter. You'll just stay the same rebellious, wise-cracking, little boy."

"I'm consistent! I don't change with the wind."

"You don't change at all! What good is that if it doesn't get you where you need to be?"

Sam got quiet. Then using a voice in which Sellia couldn't tell whether he was serious or joking he said, "I guess this is where I tell you that where I felt I needed to be was with you, spending our lives together, just a little bit at a time, fighting through the end of the world."

Sellia was quiet, too. "You don't get it at all. The rest of my life—in bulk or in installments—is still the rest of my life. There's more to this life than just surviving it. This world is going to end and we're going to die! You want to love me in hell? Is that it?"

Sam, for once, was speechless.

She kept the silence going, chewing her lips so hard that the skin beneath her nose turned white.

"So, is that what you want? To just walk off alone?" Sam finally asked.

"Yes."

"I have one last question."

"Why not?" she said, disgusted.

"Is it all right for me to be confused? Because I have no idea what's going on with you. You're on; you're off. You're black; you're white. You're at least two different people with each her own set of morality."

"Be as confused as you want," Sellia said, turning away.

"Just a thought," Sam ventured, stopping her again. "You mentioned truth earlier. What's the point of truth if it isn't true for everyone?"

Sellia was past thinking, past lectures, and past axioms. "Get away from me!" she hissed, her teeth clenched and her eyes nothing but pits. She turned on her heel and stomped off, dust from the concrete billowing after her.

She didn't look back. Sam didn't follow.

THE JOURNAL OF BOB

This is one of the main passages that depict the Omen of the Sock. Though mentions of it can be found elsewhere, this is the section that speaks upon the subject the most.

—BOBERT

Excerpt from January 13th: seven months from last entry

I sleep in my socks.

I think this may not be great etiquette, but what are you supposed to do? No matter how many blankets I have on, my bare feet are always cold. It's just better to have something on your feet. It just is.

Of course, this means every once in a while you wake up without a sock. It's kinda humiliating. A piece of clothing has been taken off you and you didn't even notice it.

Usually you can find it wrapped in the covers somewhere or at the foot of the bed. But on rare occasions, it can't be found. You're hopping around with a cold foot looking for a non-matching sock. And that is the start of a very bad day.

Chapter 12

SURRENDERING TO
BLOOD RED LIGHTS

SELLIA WAS MARCHING FURIOUSLY.
"What was the point of that?" she asked angrily.
"You had to face him. You had to stand up for yourself. For who you are. For what you believe," Bethesda said.

Sellia was in tears, "It's...horrible."

"You did what's right. You can't wait for him to agree. He can't. Can't see, can't understand. And you can't expect him to. That's his truth. And yours...yours is that way." Bethesda pointed to the west.

"Oh, yes," she said, tears drying up. "You're right."

They smiled once again in unison.

Within moments she had reached the West Side. The West Erickson Bridge had the appearance of a winter tree, bare and fruitless in its checkered cross-sections that stood stark above the waters. The waters themselves were only three feet from the bridge, making the structure look more like an enormous sidewalk.

Encouraged by the lights ahead, a waltz began playing in Sellia's head. Bethesda was conducting. The strings were crisp and the woodwinds were warm. While still conducting, Bethesda stretched his arms out to Sellia, and they waltzed across the bridge.

"One-two-three, four-five-six, one-two-three," Sellia sang softly to herself. She bent her head backward as she clung to him. Out of the corners of her eyes she watched the lights from the upside-down skyline shimmer and dance alongside her like a ballet of fireflies.

She smiled at Bethesda. Bethesda smiled back. He twisted her, moved her, spun her, and led her across the bridge. As they reached the other side, he let go and Sellia spun on her own through the streets of dust. Sellia twirled and did pirouettes by herself for moments until she looked up and realized Bethesda had gone.

She smiled and looked around, determined not to say a word, hoping to somehow sneak up on him first. She looked up the sides of the towering, illuminated buildings. She looked inside the cramped alleyways and corridors. Above and around, Bethesda was nowhere to be seen.

She walked on alone. *What is he teaching me now?* she wondered. She walked down the main street of the annexed kingdom. Each window shined a spotlight on her as she acted out her part. She strived not to wonder how important it was to be leading lady in a one-man show.

She reached the end of the street, not where it cul-de-saced or dead-ended and told drivers to U-turn their way out, but where it intersected with the ocean. *How could I not have noticed before?* she thought. She turned around to run back, but before her eyes could register, she felt cold upon her feet. Water trickled in a tiny threaded tributary toward her. It was sinister as it tried vainly to be innocent, its beautiful dance failing to be convincing.

Flash.

Flicker.

Darkness.

The lights were off. The final solace to a fallen kingdom had departed.

Bethesda laughed, but she could not hear him.

Sellia was left in the darkness. She would blink, but each time she did she noticed there was less of a difference between the insides of her eyelids and shroud of the night.

Blind, she began to listen her way around. At first there was nothing but the sound of her thoughts, forcing her to listen. They were desperate for something, but preferably someone to hold on to tightly in the night. As she remained still, her own clamor would fade into a dull buzzing.

Then she would hear it. The water. Rippling with the wind, it was a quiet and peaceful presence. More calm than she ever would have expected of impending death. This was a somber executioner, pious and reserved to fate as its minion. The peace, so morbid in its acceptance of inevitable demise, unnerved her. She fled to the bridge, the clatter of her feet and their echo off the stone walls only reminding her of how alone she was.

As she ran she again realized she could not see. The moon's muffle had now grown so tight it choked out all light flowing from the heavens. While still running, she gazed intently at the direction that she remembered that she came from.

An outline.

"Go toward it," a man-like voice commanded.

The outline was tall and broad, like a bridge, it seemed. She kept running, expecting in any moment to be listening to her bare feet echoing off of the hollow pavement of West Erickson Bridge.

Instead, the sound ended. She heard nothing more. For there was nothing more that she was running on.

Her dainty, tanned legs reached for pavement but found only more air as Sellia careened through the night into the sodden, chalky, tar-black ocean. The water, if it could be called that, was heavier here. It clung to her arms like maple syrup.

Sellia's terror, which only seconds ago had just been an inference, was now real. Death in his gentlemanly posture returned her desperate, drowning gaze with a doleful one. He was in no hurry to claim her, and so he waited.

She shook her arms but found she could not even break the surface. Her head slid down the ocean's gullet as she gasped for air the final time. She disappeared from the world, her kingdom, her mall.

She was in silence. Gooey amber seeped into her ears. All she could really hear was thick water rushing in her skull.

The soup was cold. As it encased her in its tenements, it filled her pores and embalmed her while she kept living. She thought of the fish in the aquarium and how she would now become like them. Forever preserved. Forever beautiful. She no longer felt cold. She no longer felt at all.

Her eyes remained open, drinking in the darkness. How

eternal black seemed to be. How much it hid. She wondered, while she still could think, how many others were entombed with her. How close were they? Sellia imagined her formaldehyde world blossoming with bouquets of loosely skinned corpses grinning back at her, waving toodleloo with their skeletal fingers.

Flash.

Sellia's retinas burned as red light sliced into her tomb. It arced and weaved through the darkness and vanished.

Seconds of unending darkness ended again as the light returned.

Flash.

It'll come back, she thought. *One thousand one, one thousand two, one thousand three...* she counted. And it returned for a third time, just as welcome if not more so. She felt a prodding on her back. Fingers knifing into her skin. Pain so sharp it resurrected her senses. She was feeling again.

A full hand wrapped itself around her shoulders, then another. She felt the pull and the tension as the water resisted letting her go.

She broke surface gasping and choking on air.

"My Lord! She's alive!" Streaks of brackish enamel colored her saviors. The first one appeared almost green.

"Never would've believed you, Clemsy."

"How on Earth did you see her?" A gravy yellow blur to the right of Sellia spoke.

"Get her on the boat."

Sellia was lifted into the air and set onto something comfortable. Goo still clung to her eyes, forbidding her to see her rescuers. Soft fibers touched her hand: she squeezed them with all her might. She brought the towel up to her face and wiped the filth away. She looked to her rescuers. They were the bandits. One stood over her, his helmet jutting back, his face of tire rubber smiling like a skull. His robe, devoid of color in the neutrality of the night, covered his presence, disembodying him like an apparition.

She screamed.

"Hoffman, take that stupid mask off. You're scaring the girl."

"But she could be toxic," the apparition whined.

"Take it off!"

The bandit took his mask off and his helmet and rejoined the human race.

"Are you hurt?" one asked, kneeling beside her.

"No," Sellia said, a little more trusting now that they looked human and had saved her.

"Good," he said. He turned to the others and announced, "We have our first survivor!"

They smiled and applauded, but not loudly. As she looked around she could see why. There were only six of them. Three fire-men, three members of the coast guard. They were dirty and hunkered close together. The oldest, snowy haired and with a trimmed beard, stood and turned the blood red light out. On his head he wore Sam's navy blue fedora. Even Sellia had to admit, it looked better on Sam.

The eldest sighed heavily as he looked over the sea. He looked at the sky, too, but only as someone who sees an encroaching ceiling. One of the fire-men went to talk to the old sailor. Sellia, her hearing having recently been tuned, listened.

"I think this is going to be all," the fire-man said.

"Yeah, I think so, too," the old man replied.

"What's next?"

"Float for a bit, I guess." The old salt never took his eyes from the sea.

"Float? But Murph, after this I thought you'd take us back."

"Back where? Even if we found land, there's the chance it would get swallowed, too. Best just to wait it out for now," Murph said.

"He's right," the kneeling one said. "We have to conserve gas."

"How about we take a vote?" Hoffman asked.

"Again?" grumbled Murph.

"We don't need a vote," the kneeling man said.

"You don't speak for everyone, Clemsy," Hoffman said. "All who think we need to return to the station, raise your hands!" As Hoffman said it, two hands raised to join his: a member of the coast guard and another fire-man.

"The station is underwater," Murph said.

"We don't know that," Hoffman snapped.

"Listen, there's not a good reason for us not just to wait here." Clemsy stood to face Hoffman.

"But…things aren't getting any better around here," Sellia said. "Maybe we can find some land untouched somewhere."

"Ma'am, things aren't going to be better any place else," Murph said, sounding as if he was trying to be comforting. "It is going to be like this until the end. This boat; this group—it's all we're going to have." Even through the mud that caked Sellia's appearance, Murph seemed to be able to tell she used to be a moneyed individual. "It may sound mundane, but that's life. You can hold out for hope, but it's false. Just accept it for what it is."

"Call a dime a dime," another chided.

Sellia's eyes watered to Murph's stark vision.

"Now, that doesn't mean we won't take care of you and each other as we wait," Murph said quickly.

"Wait for what? For rescue?" Sellia asked.

"We *are* the rescue," Murph said. "At least we were. There's no one coming."

Sellia was now deathly quiet, realizing she had been saved from one fate in order to be offered to another.

After several minutes struggling with accepting the bitter pill, she said, "What about the monster?" As she said it, she wanted to stop herself, knowing how silly it sounded.

"The what?" Clemsy asked.

"I know; it's a big fish with ten fins, but I saw it devour a man." Sellia attempted to sound knowledgeable in an attempt to make up for the story's unbelievability.

"Now, we did see a big fish," Murph said, leaning up against the steering wheel. "It was longer than the boat. It didn't bother us though, ma'am."

"Didn't look wide enough to have swallowed a man," one of the members of the coast guard said.

"It didn't…Well, I don't know if it *ate* him, exactly. It *sliced* him. Like a knife, or a pair of garden shears."

There was silence as the crew digested the image, their grim faces broadcasting their grimmer imaginations.

"Well, I'm not a sailor, but I've never heard of an animal that kills without eating. Nothing kills just for the thrill of it," Clemsy said softly.

"It kinda helped us, as I recall," Murph said. "Cleared some seaweed and some brush for us in our path. Maybe it even ate a few of the more troublesome fish for us, sharks and the like."

"Do sharks come up this way?" Hoffman asked. Someone elbowed him.

"What we're saying is that it's worked in conjunction with us so far, and it doesn't look like it will give us much trouble," Clemsy clarified.

"Oh," Sellia said trying to push the image of a dismembered boB out of her mind.

Slowly everyone on the boat began to grow quiet as one by one they noticed a sound. Upon closer inspection it was a voice.

"Looks like you get your way after all, ma'am. We get to burn up more gas," Murph said as he cranked the engine.

"Let's hope this isn't a wild goose chase again."

"Yeah, Clemsy claimed he heard a boat earlier."

"No more strange noises for me. Phantom boats, phantom noises; mission is getting spookier all the time," Clemsy said.

Sellia watched as the stern shot a stream of white water out behind them. Clemsy handed her a yellow lifejacket and strapped her in it.

The voice was louder now. There was a melody to it, though it was sung purely a cappella:

The trees up north are afraid of dying,
The trees down south are tired of crying.
And me, oh me, I'm too sick of trying,
But I found a way to my bustling home.

It was Sam.
Naturally, thought Sellia.

Sam had found himself a tree and was leaning on one of its thick branches, feet propped up on the trunk; the stalk of it rising up out of the water.

"Hello, there. Are you in need of a rescue?" Sam asked.

The fire-men ignored the question. "Who can climb up there and get him?"

"Careful. It could be shallow here," another said.

"Sellia? What are you doing riding with your bandits? Your tastes really have changed," Sam said. The boat parked underneath the tree.

"I can climb up," Hoffman offered.

"Is that my hat?" Sam gawked.

"No need," Clemsy said to Hoffman. He snatched the hat off of Murph's head. "Looks like it!" Clemsy yelled to Sam.

"Toss it to me!" Sam yelled.

"No, I might miss and it'd hit the water! Better come and get it."

Sam seemed to change his mind about his hat and went back to singing.

If I had a Savior,
Would He tell me what to do?
Would I go to Heaven later,
If I promised to be true?

"Sam," Sellia said, "come down. I'm sorry about earlier." There was an obligatory weight to her voice.

Sam slanted his eyes at her. *He must've caught it*, she thought.

"C'mon down, son," Murph said. "City's going down."

"Yeah, but is your way really any better than any one else's? I might just be better off on my own."

Sellia grimaced as she heard him recite his mantra. She took a running start for the side of the boat and leapt up, pushing Sam off of his perch. Sam plummeted into the water. Sellia, however, landed very gracefully back in the boat.

"Lady, any one of us could've done that," Hoffman said.

Clemsy fished him out of the water. Sam was shivering. Hoffman brought Sam a trench coat. Sam wrapped Hoffman's plastic yellow fire-man's garb around him and stiffly outstretched his hand to Murph.

"Hat," was all Sam said. Murph obliged him. Sam positioned his old friend back on his head. Murph then turned off the engine, allowing them to drift.

Sam sat down in the stern of the boat. Sellia sat down on the side.

"We match," Sam said, pointing from his yellow trench coat to her yellow life jacket.

Sellia said nothing. She looked down at her hands. She glanced over her shoulder. She rocked in place. For a second she caught his eyes.

"The silent treatment only works when it doesn't drive yourself crazy," Sam laughed. Sellia violently looked away once again. "So why'd you go over to the 'enemy.'"

She looked at him squarely, "I just want to survive."

"I'd be picky about how I'd do it," he smiled. "After all, you're going to have to live with it."

She grimaced at him. "You disapprove of my choices again?"

"Maybe not. But you shouldn't have saved me. You should've respected my decision. I respected yours when you left." He sat, contented, by himself, glancing genuinely toward the horizon.

They sat with each other in their newfound truce until light peeked across the ocean. It did so slowly, as the clouds still clogged the sky. When the dingy dawn was fully upon them, the coast guard seemed to realize in their sad eyes that once again they had been cheated out of another colorful sunrise.

Meanwhile, hunger had come to Sellia. She sat still wrestling with it, losing with each attempt. Each time Sellia opened her mouth to say something, she lapsed into guilt. At last she could stand it no more. "Does anyone have any food?"

"I got some crackers," Hoffman offered. He dug inside his suspendered trousers and brought out a crumbling package of orange-colored peanut butter crackers.

"You're going to have to share that," Murph warned. Each member of the crew extended expectant hands toward Hoffman. Clemsy relieved him of the crackers and began dividing it among the fire-men, the survivors, and the coastguard.

Sellia looked at her share of the compromise and with a single swallow felt it disappear into her vacuous stomach. Her stomach roared louder in retaliation for the tease of food. She apologized to it and tried to turn her attention to the horizon.

Fog had settled onto the early morning sea, obscuring the trunks and peaks of the city's buildings. From where she sat, Sellia could see a bit of the office district that had been drenched by the ensuing waters. Even further uphill was a church sanctuary. Balancing quaint with regal, it boasted both stained glass windows and a towering cross-tipped steeple. It was much smaller than the office buildings surrounding it and sat alone above them on its hill.

"God, what a mess," Murph said to no one in particular. "We're gonna get 'em back for this."

"Got anyone in mind?" Clemsy asked.

"Terrorists! Man, don't you know that? It had to be them!"

"You guys don't even know what happened. No one does," Clemsy said.

"Looks like we got a dove here, boys," Murph laughed.

"Actually, I saw what looked like a husk of some sort of bomb," Sam said.

"Could be, could be," Clemsy said.

"Would you look at that? Even when confronted with proof, he won't do anything!" Murph said.

"What would you have me do? Go down to my personal, flooded war room and push the button to blow more people up?" Clemsy asked.

"Hey, hey look," Sellia said pointing out over the ocean. At first Sam looked at her as if she was pretending to see something just to stop the argument.

"Get ready to crank that motor again, Murph. We may have more survivors," Clemsy said. A boat-like structure teetered on the seas in the shrouded distance. A water-churning, gear-gnawing sound erupted from the stern as Murph cranked the engine.

Murph took them at a careful pace as they attempted to dock parallel to the red-and-white boat. Sellia looked quickly to Sam as she realized exactly whose boat they were disturbing.

"Hello?" Hoffman asked the boat as they pulled up closer. "Is there anyone over there?" Sellia realized for the first time that the boat had a cabin. *I didn't know Bob had been so well off,* she thought.

"Attention!" the boat roared back in Bobert's voice with scratchy and grainy sibilance. "Announcing the leader of the world's faith, the truth speaker, and naysayer to Wallace: boB!" The cabin doors swung open and Rab walked out on deck, Bobacita tucked in his scrawny arms and her chin riding on his bony shoulder. The long train of a bathrobe followed after him.

"Greetings, nonbelievers! I bring you tidings of hope from our great provider," Rab yelled.

"What the devil?" Murph said. The rest were speechless.

THE JOURNAL OF BOB

Excerpt from August 5ᵗʰ: six months prior to previous entry

Jon brought Leesa, Karen, and Jeremy to me today and said they had something to say to me. I expected them to complain that I didn't put the vacuum in the right closet, so I was surprised to hear them say...

"We heard about what Wallace did to you," Leesa said.

"Um, what was that exactly?" I asked.

"Put the heat on until one of you had to quit," Jeremy said.

"You guys are like Romeo and Juliet," Karen said.

"Me and Meredith?"

"Yeah, and that makes Wallace...well, the bad guy," Jeremy said.

"Well, there is no 'me and Meredith,' so it's OK," I clarified.

"That's awful! You want to talk about it?" Karen said.

"That's not what we're here about guys," Jon reminded them.

"Oh, yeah. What do you want us to do to him?" Karen said

"Wallace. How do you want us to get him back?" Jeremy said.

"I don't want to get back at anybody!" I said.

"But Bob, how long 'til Wallace gets one of us?" Leesa asked.

"Listen, if you want to prevent him from bullying you, there's only one thing to do—quit," I said. "Yeah, we're each about a week from that ourselves," Jon said. "So Bob, we were wondering, how sick of this job are you?"

* * * *

Bob's original disciples are a disreputable bunch, drawn to Bob's own distaste of Wallace and his battle with the dark manager. Together, they follow Bob to dethrone him.

—BOBERT

Chapter 13

THE BOSOM OF MOSES

"**W**E KNOW WHO YOU ARE. THE FIRE-MEN!" RAB raised his stringy arms and wailed with a feigned deep voice. "Those who would prefer to take people away from the city and its problems rather than fix it. You don't really care to change the world, just escape it. But worse, you don't try because you have neglected the great teachings of *him*! Change from your wicked ways!"

"Change!" Bobacita chanted.

"Um, yeah," Clemsy said, ignoring him. "Would you like to come aboard? Or would you like to follow us to a safer coordinate?"

"How are you on gas?" Hoffman asked the Bobbers.

Sam looked to Sellia. "The gun," he whispered.

"Wait, wait, wait…" Murph said. "*They…have a gun?*"

"Worldly cares! Bobbers, show them their fate if they fail to convert." Berty hopped up from the floor and Bobert came out of the cabin as each of them threw a balled up package at the coast guard boat.

"Grenades!" Murph yelled, ducking on the floor.

Sam and Sellia watched as rolled socks hit the deck and bounced.

"Bad Times!" the Bobbers screamed.

"It is but an omen. An omen of harsher times to come for you! A sign," Rab the boB announced.

Murph clunked around the boat over to Clemsy. "They have guns!"

"Um-hmm," Clemsy agreed.

"So what are we gonna do?" Murph urged.

Sellia watched as the Bobbers sat down on the far side of their boat. They sat as a panel of judges in front of them.

Clemsy leaned out across to the Bobbers. "Is it true you have firearms?"

"If you heard it from those two, you may not want to be too trusting. They turned on us. They're responsible for the death of our first leader," Berty said.

Clemsy looked at Sam and Sellia. "You killed their leader?"

"You were one of them?" Murph asked.

"*She* was one of them. I was divisive," Sam said, pointing to Sellia.

Sellia was watching Berty. A soggy woolen afghan covered her lap. A long, telltale object was concealed beneath it.

"Is that true?" Clemsy kept prodding Sellia. "Who are they?"

"Don't trifle with us, fire-men! Or we shall smite you like Bob smit Wallace," Rab, the new boB shouted, "with a high heel and a shoe-horn!"

Sellia watched as the sailors huddled near an open strong box at the bow. Instinctively, she backed up to the side.

"Smit?" Sam asked aloud.

"Listen, I don't mean to come off harsh. I just would like anything you could tell me," Clemsy said to Sellia.

There was a loud noise. It could have been a gun, or thunder, or the ships banging up against each other. But in the next second Sellia was sprayed by Clemsy's blood as he fell to the floor. The red liquid seemed to dance in an arc as it careened through the air. Sellia jerked her head back in fear, disgust, surprise, and revulsion at the gruesome ballet. She fell over the side.

The coast guard returned fire with their guns from the strong box. A Bobber, bloodied and deceased, fell from the opposing boat. Sellia, as she floated away unharmed from the scrape, could see Sam in the confusion. He ducked and debated where he should be, not that he had any affinity for either side. For a moment their eyes met. The next moment Sam was in the water.

Luckily for Sam, the water had a thinner consistency than the sludge near the West Side. He bobbed through the water to her, his eyes eager for the safety of consistency.

Blood poured from the two boats as the standoff continued. Sellia tried to look away, but as the red meandered its way down the sides and into the water, it created a presence she could not escape; she was swimming among the dead. Sellia began to panic, flailing her arms about, even managing for a moment while wearing her life vest to sink beneath the blood-filled water. Sam swam to her.

"It's OK, it's..." Sam said. She clung to him. With her weight he sank down, getting a taste of the rusty blood himself. She was too heavy for him, and he for her. Once she saw she was drowning him, Sellia let go, allowing him to tread back to the surface, hat still firmly in place upon his head.

Now, both floating and relatively calm, they looked back to the skirmish. Ten leathery flags of distress arose from the waters as Moses arrived and began eating indiscriminately from the bodies of Bobbers, the fire-men, and coast guard.

Sam and Sellia frantically searched the foggy horizon for their options of escape as their predator began running out of defendants.

The church on the hill was the last piece of reachable land yet untouched by the ensuing waters. Sam and Sellia swam to the shore. Sellia tried to push back the thought of being swallowed together with Sam in a vortex of teeth.

Sam caught the shoreline with his lanky arms and began pulling himself up, dragging Sellia with him. She clutched his arm so tightly it cut off the blood flow. Between the cold water and his human tourniquet, Sam's arm had become purple and quite possibly numb. Sellia at last let go and they ran toward the broad wooden doors, nudging them open with shoulders and momentum. Once inside, they searched for a way to lock it, anything to bar the doors.

"Don't lock it," a voice said from the altar. "Someone else may come."

"Moses is coming!" Sellia shouted. Sam found a way to switch the deadbolt on.

"No, I don't believe he gets a second coming," the voice smiled. The warmth. The joviality. Sam turned around. It was the bum, his fishing cap still resting lopsided on his aged head.

"You're alive!" Sam yelled and ran up to him. Once there, Sam could not decide whether to shake his hand or hug him. The bum decided for Sam, pulling the boy close to him and wrapping Sam in dirty, but warm, be-trenchcoated arms.

Sellia looked around the room and took in the expansive chapel. It was brilliant and well taken care of—polished wood cross in the back; gleaming banisters; marble pulpit; colorful stained glass windows depicting the Creation, Abraham and Isaac, the baptism of Christ, the Sermon on the Mount, the Crucifixion, and the Resurrection. But there was one thing incredibly wrong about this church.

There were obscenities written everywhere. On the ceiling, the floor, across the windows, over the door, behind the pulpit. Innuendo had dried on every surface.

Even Sellia, who only thought of church as a runway for her Sunday dresses, was appalled. "Oh, my…Did you do this?" she was actually angry.

"No," the bum smiled. It was a peculiar smile. The smile did not seem to register the blasphemies behind him.

"This doesn't offend you?" Sellia asked.

"My God is bigger than a building. Or a symbol. Or a person. It shocks me that someone would do this, but it can't possibly offend me. Maybe if my faith were in these pews, then yes. But, well, you get the idea."

Sam sat down in one of the pews and looked forward. "What were you doing in here?"

"Talking. To God."

"Praying?" Sellia specified.

"Sure," the bum shrugged. "It was more of a conversation. I wanted peace. He gave it to me. And then you came and brought me some company," he smiled again.

"Yeah, I do that, too. I talk to God like a conversation," Sellia said.

"How about you?" the bum asked Sam.

"Well, I'm a heretic," Sam laughed sheepishly. "I was just kicked out of a religion."

"Hey, don't feel bad. Some heretics are great people. I'm a disciple of a heretic," the bum said. "Some religions are so focused on enforcing laws they forget the spirit of them. Laws are important. They guide us, they set us on the right path. In the end we're all guilty of breaking them. And then death comes. But any time man puts laws above God, he defeats the purpose of religion."

"Which begs the question—" Sam began.

"Relationship. That's the purpose. A relationship with our Creator."

"Like a lover?" Sellia asked.

"Yeah," the bum said. "I bet He misses us. Just like a young couple suffering from their first few months apart. Why not that ravenously?"

Sellia smiled. The smile was genuine, all plastic wrapping peeled off, all gaudy makeup smeared away.

There was a tremor as a loud noise shook the building.

"Moses again," Sam said. "I think we should be able to keep him out a bit longer if we jam the doorway with a pew." Sam got up from his seat and began pushing one of the back pews toward the door. The bum went to help.

Sellia watched as they barricaded the door. She felt frail and scared knowing that only a few wooden planks stood between her and judgment.

"Lord, please protect me from harm. This is not how I want to die," she prayed.

Bethesda came. "I will. I have much greater plans for you."

"You do?" she asked excitedly.

"Of course," he laughed. "I won't let you die with a boy and a bum."

"Thank you, Lord," she prayed.

"You're welcome," said Bethesda.

The bum came back. He walked slowly and sat down for a moment. He spoke so normally she thought for a moment he was talking to Sam. But he was too quiet for that. After another moment of listening she realized that he was praying for them.

She looked back at her selfish prayer and her selfish god and wondered if she and the bum could even be praying to the same person.

The door quaked again.

"He's coming!" Sam yelled.

"All right," the bum cleared his throat. "You two need to get to the roof."

"The roof? How?" Sam looked around, realizing the sanctuary comprised the entirety of the church. There were no doors marked Exit with little pictures of stairs.

The bum looked up to the front of the church. Above the cross was a circular stained glass window depicting the Ascension, a red-and-white stoic Christ levitating among pious disciples. At first, Sellia only thought the bum was being religious, especially when she heard the bum say, "Gather around the cross." But he continued with, "Climb up it. I'll help you."

Sellia went first. The bum squatted on the floor and lifted her to the right branch of the cross.

"Now it's your turn," he said to Sam. Sam stepped on the bum's palms and slowly found himself being lifted to the branch.

"Now what?" Sellia huffed over her shoulder.

"Hang on, but be ready to climb through that window," the bum said. He knelt at the foot of the cross and began unscrewing it from the floor, his calloused fingers squeezing each screw out. As he did, an innocent trickle of water began to meander through the blockade and into the sanctuary.

Sellia noticed the cross had lost a great deal of its stability and was beginning to tilt. The bum pressed up against the cross, his back to the door. His head was at Sam and Sellia's ankles. He bent his knees as he tilted forward. "Slowly, slowly," the bum wheezed. The cross leaned toward the wall and at last came to rest against the circular window.

As the cross shifted, Sellia saw that her hands went from barely holding on to the ledge to now her elbows resting at ease on the incline. She lifted herself up with no difficulty. Seeing that

Sam had already lifted himself up, she nodded for him to smash open the window.

Sam seemed to muse over how would be the best way to make his exit before finally removing his hat, placing his fist inside it, and punching the stained glass window into colorful splinters. He attempted to brush off the sill with his hat as well, but there was very little room for the glass to collect. He put his foot on the sill and reached toward the roof.

"Sellia!" Sam called. Sellia lay motionless on the cross, silently wondering about the bum and listening to the faint sounds of water filling the church.

"I'm staying," the bum said, winking at her. "We're going to be all right."

Sellia mouthed "thank you" and leapt out the window to Sam's waiting hand. Sam lifted her up. Sellia almost tripped as she landed on the roof of the church. As she looked down to where she came from, she backed away in horror. "The water has already gone past the land. Another few feet and it will be past the window!"

Sam was looking around. The only sights left in the city were the rooftops, steeples, and domes. The foliage from distant trees made it appear as if grass was growing from the sea.

The sea itself was still as black as it had been for five days. In the distance the remains of the coast guard ship and the Bowmaster were indistinguishable in the tar-smelted sea. Sellia watched as the boats were tossed in the black soup, as if the water were being stirred by someone at an enormous kettle.

Then someone, or at least the spoon, showed itself.

Moses rose from the flood. Its skin was a blotchy gray and white with an enamel of slime and salt water, which dripped from its overly long snout and each of its visible fins. As it thrashed its narrow head violently, it displayed its massive smile of needle-like teeth. It had pink, membranous eyes that looked more like pockets of puss that any organ, be it a fish organ or otherwise. There were no pupils in its eyes, just hollow mirrors that served to reflect its victims' frightened faces.

Sam pushed Sellia to the ground as the leviathan opened its jaws. Sellia wondered, as she knelt under Sam, how long she would have to wait before she felt those scissor-like jaws on her skin. The moment lingered. The longer it lasted, the more Sellia wondered if she was already dead.

She looked up. The jaws were open, bits of flesh and meat clinging to the roof of its mouth. The throat reeked of rancid blood. The creature was frozen in place. The waves were as still as glass and the wind neglected to move.

Time had stopped around them.

THE JOURNAL OF BOB

Excerpt from August 20th: fifteen days from previous entry

On an average day there are anywhere from fifteen to twenty workers in Archer's department store. Generally, there are about two to a department, but some days we do just fine with one. Today was an average day, but I don't believe any of us will ever remember it that way.

Business was steady, leading up to the rush of Labor Day weekend in a few weeks. At twelve o'clock Jon came over to me.

"You're going to do it, right? We talked about this. I know you're nervous, but so was—"

"Yeah, yeah, so was Julius Caesar every time he went before the senate. Do you know what happened to Julius Caesar at the senate?"

"You won't be betrayed. We got your back."

"I've been practicing my 'Et tu's' just in case." I exhaled and marched off.

"You're doing it now?"

"No time like the present."

"We need time to mobilize."

"You mobilize. I'm talking to Wallace." I marched across the floor toward Wallace's ironclad door. After pounding on it for several seconds, a scowling Wallace opened the door.

"Why aren't you in your department?" Wallace asked.

"I quit. Just wanted to tell you in person."

"You're supposed to put in your two weeks' notice."

"Then I won't call and ask for a recommenda-tion," I said as I turned around and walked away.

He followed me.

"You think you're pretty smart, you and that fresh little thing you used to be so cozy with. In-store relationships are frowned upon. You're lucky I didn't report the two of you to corporate."

I ignored him and took the long way out, passing through the dresses and lingerie.

"I knew it! You're a pervert. There you are!" Wallace laughed.

As I passed I made eye contact with Karen and Susan. Now I needed Leesa; I found her in the children's department.

"Aw, no. Children?" Wallace said. "I see how you are. You really are sick aren't you?" Customers were starting to stare and I was turning red. It's OK. Let em' stare, I thought. Let em' all see him for who he is.

Leesa joined me the rest of the way as I marched toward the exit. There we were joined by Jon, Susan, Jake, Karen, and about seven other Archer's employees.

I mean ex-employees. We walked out together and went and saw a movie.

"Bob! Come back here, Bob!" Wallace yelled. I didn't like the way he said my name; I spat out of just hearing it come out of his foul mouth.

"Let him run that store all by himself," we said.

Wallace ended up closing the store early. I don't know when he's going to be able to open it back up again.

* * * *

In addition to being the key passage for the confrontation with Wallace, this entry also gives us our most often used custom.

We do not know the tone of voice nor the inflection Wallace used when he said Bob's name, therefore out of reverence and not wanting to displease Bob, we rarely if ever speak his name aloud.

—BOBERT

Chapter 14

THE POLITICS OF SATAN

"No, I told you before. You can't kill them," The Shining Man said, walking along the gold cobblestones of paradise.

"I was hoping You had changed Your mind," The Fish Eater growled. He adjusted one of his many masks, its appearance grotesque and demonic; a gnarled face of wood with a yawning mouth of teeth and a pronounced tongue.

"You know I see right through you." The Shining Man turned and smiled at His adversary.

Looking away while still turning myriad masks toward his Enemy, The Fish Eater asked, "Can I wound them?"

"No," The Shining Man said.

"Then what was the point of being able to wipe out all those fire-men and coast guard and my own private cult if these two always walk away unscathed?" The Fish Eater was past his boiling point. "Give me something. I want her!"

The Shining Man only shook His head.

"She's lost and he's misguided. Neither knows what they want, so they can't want You!" The Fish Eater said.

"How do you know what they want?" He answered.

The Fish Eater looked down while still tilting a dozen angry faces at The Shining Man. "Insanity," The Fish Eater said.

"No," He said.

"Disease. A plague. Let me cover her with boils. Make her peel her perfect skin right off her spoiled little face."

"No," He said again.

"Famine! She's never known hunger! I'll make her try to eat the sludge off the water!"

"They're on a roof, Beelzebub. They don't have any food. I'd think you could wait for nature to run its course," The Shining Man said.

The Fish Eater was quiet, disguising fear in his silence.

The Shining Man smiled again.

"Then let me torment her," The Fish Eater said. "Mentally. Attack her mind. Accuse her. Bring her down. I do it every minute, and I know You'll let me do it now. Temptation and desire are mine to paint with and my tools to alter what You create."

"Finish what you started," The Shining Man said.

The phantom prince smiled beneath his headdress and descended through the firmament. He sliced through the gray clouds like a dark star, fast and terrible, yet he landed as gracefully as a dove on the cathedral steeple. He placed his bare hand on the cross and rubbed it. A thundering cackle echoed in his helmet. He slowly turned to Sam and Sellia, who were still clutching each other as he descended the steeple like a palatial staircase.

He stood over them, eight feet tall and growing larger in their minds. The cloaks and robes and jewels and necklaces that were pale and pointless in the plenty of the celestial heavens were now glittering enough to blot out the sun. And with no sun to be seen, their shimmer replaced it.

His robes were of satin, linen, and silk, adorned with every color and hemmed to perfection. As they draped across the chapel roof, they never mussed, never dirtied.

Necklaces from Persia, Tunisia, Taiwan, and Capri all swung in a tantalizing gait around his neck. Themes of silver, gold, obsidian, amethyst, and ivory echoed in his rings, bracelets, necklaces, and masks.

His masks were from every tribe and religion that had paid homage to him since the beginning of time. They were piled and assorted on top of, next to, adjacent, and parallel to one another. There was not a place a person could stand near him and not fear they were being watched by those endless eyes.

"Are you a god?" Sellia asked.

"Yes," The Fish Eater replied. "I am."

"You look like a tiki torch," Sam said, biting his bottom lip. He kept his arms around Sellia. He kept her safe. "All you're missing—"

"—is a roasted pig? An apple in my mouth? Maybe a pineapple impaled on one of my horns?"

Sam was speechless as he heard his words stolen from his throat.

"Or had you even made up your mind yet what your clever insult would be? Do you think that your human insults affect me? That by telling me to 'Go to hell,' I actually will? So keep on stabbing at me. You're not hitting any flesh," The Fish Eater snarled. "I've been laughing at you all along. Look to your side, and you'll see your 'courage.'"

Sam was surrounded on either side by hairy, bulbous demons without eyes or ears but with chattering lips that whispered every insult or witty retort he had ever credited to himself. Scared and frightened by his own ugliness, Sam pressed his hands to his face, where he found no reprieve either. He released his hands and stared at the ground.

"Stop," Sam finally said.

The Fish Eater paused for only a second before continuing, "Getting more courageous now? Are you sure you're not getting your lines fed to you by my minions?"

"You bully me because you're afraid of me."

"Afraid? I am a god. There is no fear. In me are no emotions you could ever know."

"No emotions? Everything I feel. *Everything.* Envy, jealousy, cowardice, these emotions define you! You push feeling and wield them because that is all you are."

The Fish Eater gnashed his teeth, white and blue blazes licking out of his fingers.

The next thing The Fish Eater saw was The Shining Man standing before him. When he realized he was back in heaven and that the Son of Man was not back on Earth, he sighed relief.

"We just went over this. You can't hurt Sam, either," The Shining Man said.

"What?" The Fish Eater hyperventilated.

"You can't have Sam. He's mine." The Shining Man smiled as brightly as any proud Papa.

"What can I do?" The Fish Eater asked. "What will You let me do?"

"What you were intending. Do what you like to their minds. Do not harm them."

"Confuse, distract, judge, condemn. I can do all of these things?"

"The better question is, Why are you wasting your time talking to Me?" The Shining Man said. He had an air of finality about Him. The way the Alpha and Omega was starting to sound like a man finishing a sentence sent fear into him. The Fish Eater vanished back to Earth faster than before and with far less grace.

THE JOURNAL OF BOB

Excerpt from March 27th: seven months from previous entry

Final Entry

I finally decided to take Melvin's advice today and see the office building he works in.

"Come on, man. You don't have to work there, too. But you've already too long searching for a job. Just come; I'll show you around. We'll have lunch."

At Kilma-Teck, Melvin works as a mail carrier. As he showed me today, he spends about three hours in the basement sorting the mail. Then he gets to stretch his legs and push the mail cart around.

He makes it look like a lot of fun, but I'm going to have to pass. I would like to work with my friend, but I'm not certain that I wouldn't get sick of him after too long in the dungeon of this place.

I'm resting here by one of the cubicles while Melvin makes his rounds with the carrier. After he gets off work I guess we'll—

* * * *

This is all that we have regarding the final entry of Bob's journal. After its mysterious ending, it is anyone's guess what happened.

—BOBERT

Chapter 15
THE DEVIL, YOURSELF

THE CONVERSATION BETWEEN THE FISH EATER and the Creator of the world had taken only a moment. With the trip back taking a nanosecond and the trip there taking no time at all, the entirety of time The Fish Eater had gone missing averaged out to be about one tick of the clock.

Sam had blinked at that moment and Sellia had not been interested enough to notice.

"Away," The Fish Eater said, and pushed Sam to the seclusion of an island eleven miles away, a gravel-covered mound of dirt in the water. He was safe, but he had no Sellia to comfort and no devil to annoy.

"Good morning," The Fish Eater started.

"Good morning," Sellia replied, eyeing his jewelry. She reached out for it like a kitten would for a piece of yarn.

"You like them?" The Fish Eater milked his own rhetorical question. As he removed a necklace containing an obsidian stone in a silver setting, dropping it in her lap, another appeared on his neck.

"So beautiful," Sellia said.

"Tempered. Like the earth itself. Raw beauty. It is so much a part of the thing, it is no longer just a description. It is a definition," The Fish Eater said.

Sellia nodded. She held the stone in one hand as she played with the chain in the other.

"But you don't understand what I'm saying. Not really. Because you're not beautiful anymore, are you?"

She looked up at him. No man, not even in the past few days, had ever called her anything less than beautiful. She unfolded her legs and stood up in protest. "Yes, I am."

"Where is your proof? Where are your throngs of adoring public? Where are your servants? Where are your *men*?"

"Well, Sam—"

"Oh, Sam! *Sam* is not a man. *Sam* is a boy," The Fish Eater mocked. "You used Sam as a consolation because you have no proof!"

"I—"

"That's all Sam was to you! Just proof that you were beautiful. You just admitted it. Out of the abundance of the heart the mouth speaks."

"You just said—"

Again he cut her off mid syllable. "You spoiled brat. Wasn't Sam enough? Who is boB...and Rab?"

"They're both nice guys, really, but—"

"But they're still worth treating Sam like sludge? I see. Yes, you are *so* beautiful. Didn't anyone tell you that real beauty comes from within? That you're only as beautiful as you treat people."

She could not look at him anymore. She walked five steps to the end of the roof. But her feet did not take her anywhere, and she was still standing beside her accuser.

"boB and his lackeys were so caught up by your superficial 'beauty' that they targeted Sam. They sniped at him, up close and at a distance, just to have you. And poor Sam! Why was he dragged there into that position? Yes, because of your 'beauty.' Sam went through hell for you." The Fish Eater was smiling under his mask, and his voice was starting to show it. "But that's only figurative. Guess who really went through hell?"

A mist spilled out of The Fish Eater's cloak and poured out into the form of a vortex. A stench of sulfur wafted out of the black mist, as the broad frame of boB was shown walking out. His flesh was peeling and his entire body was blackened, but he didn't seem all that gruesome. Violently, he dropped to the ground and wriggled. And screamed. He screamed much like Sellia remembered he did before he died. Fire from elsewhere washed over his body as even boB's contusions went into convulsions.

"Hello, Melvin. What do you see?" A chain formed around boB's neck and led all the way back to the crafty hand of The Fish Eater. Sellia wasn't permitted to close her eyes as the skin of the man was burned away like excess plastic. Water filled her eyes from tears, sweat, and the heat of the fire.

"I see darkness!" boB yelled again. He wailed in a sort of croon fitting for a wolf. The sounds coming from boB no longer were regal but primal, of a guttural quality, revealing base, instinctual fear and self-loathing.

"He may seem like he's here to you, but he hasn't escaped Gehenna!" The Fish Eater said in an aside to Sellia before turning back to boB.

"Melvin. Melvin? Are you listening? Are you bored?"

Fire consumed boB as he screamed even louder. Skull was beginning to become visible.

"Sellia is here. I know you can't see her, but I know you have a message for her. What would you like me to tell her?"

A slew of profanities blasted Sellia from boB's mouth, slapping her across the face. But it was just the preamble. Soon boB said, "Send her here! Send her here!"

Sellia was on her knees, crying as boB lay burning.

"These are your crimes, Sellia," The Fish Eater said. He was suddenly joined by twelve other men. All of them were dressed to go out on a date, more specifically: a date with Sellia.

"Not you," she said to none of them in particular. She was equally reluctant to see any of them, especially since they were the chosen jurors.

The first one was the youngest, sixteen and wearing a blue pinstriped suit and a gold tie that his parents had probably picked out. In his right hand he held a corsage. "I was waiting hours. When were you going to come?"

The next was at least a dozen years older, just by the way he dressed. He wore a loosened buttoned-up shirt, but he looked at home in it, as if he were wearing a nightshirt. "I traveled all this way just to tell you I love you."

Another was in his mid twenties, blonde, cocky, and confident, just like her. "I could've been so happy just being miserable
with you. Why couldn't—"

"I see now! You love yourself, don't you?" The Fish Eater
laughed. "Tell me. Do you still?"

boB still wailed in the background. The obsidian necklace she
wore looped itself around her neck. It was heavy. Its chains grew
longer. It came alive like a serpent, and its coils swarmed across
and overtop of her as The Fish Eater spoke again. "I wonder what
these men saw in you? I wonder if they'd still see it? If they were
really here. But they're not. I am," it said. "I will be here for you.
I will take it all away. I will be your lover. I am all you need." He
raised his masks up just enough to reveal two perfect, symmet-
rical, red, valentine lips. He drew closer. A breath away from her
face and close enough to draw her to him, he waited.

She whispered faintly, and had it been any other word he
might not have heard her.

"Jesus," Sellia said.

The headdresses came down upon his head and covered his
face once again. He backed away. He had to.

As he rebounded back, he nodded to another that then stepped
forward.

"Here I am," Bethesda said. "You sent for me."

His presence was different somehow from the one she perceived
when she spoke with the bum.

"Save me," she said.

"Surely," and a gleaming broadsword appeared in Bethesda's
hands. He brandished it toward The Fish Eater. "Back, demon!
Vile thing."

"Oh no!" The Fish Eater wailed, his sardonic tone only barely
concealed. He pretended to cower, but even in his cowering he
still held his head higher than Bethesda's.

"Get away from the girl and go back to your pit!" Bethesda
handed The Fish Eater the sword. The Fish Eater took the sword
and cradled the blade in his armpit, between his robes and
his body.

"I'm slain. Oh, but I'm slain!" The Fish Eater had executed a Vaudeville-grade pratfall there on the roof of the church.

Bethesda wrapped his arms around her. He was overly warm and sticky, "There, there, child. I have you."

"You have me?" Sellia said.

"Like always," Bethesda said.

"Then what's your name?"

Bethesda was quiet as he worked up the courage to pronounce it. The Fish Eater was on his feet in an instant.

"It's enough that you know it," Bethesda explained.

"Jesus," she said louder. "Save me!"

The Fish Eater reared back again. "No! Never! This is not His world," The Fish Eater swore. "This is my world. I took it a long time ago. Those were the rules. I get what I want, and I get you!"

THE JOURNAL OF BOB

The missing entry after the final entry.

Entry from March 29th:

I didn't want to write this. But I think it's the best way to honor my friend. Bob came here to visit me a few days ago. While he was here, something, an explosion, a bomb, an act of God happened. And it killed him.

No, no.

When it happened, I was tossed to the floor and the mail carrier was sent a few paces in front of me. Once I realized that the ceiling had caved in, I saw that a large beam had struck Jerry's desk, who had left for a job in Belfast a week ago. Bob had been sitting there. The beam had him pinned against the ground. He was still breathing, mumbling, turning his head back and forth as people screamed around us. People were running everywhere. All running away. No one came to help.

He kept mumbling, kept talking about fishing and our lunch, and about how he shouldn't have left Wallace or led the walk-out and about Meredith. He was in such pain. I couldn't move him. And so many people had just left.

No one was around.

I had no choice. I put my hands, which were so much larger than his face, over his nose and mouth, and I kept them there. I kept pushing until there was nothing left. Until he had no pain.

I can't believe I did it.

I can't let anyone read this.

Chapter 16

REALLY ISN'T THE END
OF THE WORLD

THE SKY QUAKED AND UNPARALLELED LIGHT SHONE as the Son came out of place in the sky and began moving toward the Earth. As the clouds peeled back, the Son on His white horse touched down onto the water of the flooded city. His brilliance reflected off the water and lit up the city. The world was yellow again.

Thousands of other white horses rampaged down upon the earth. They were warriors with gleaming swords, royal robes, and perfect new bodies. But out of all of the holy invaders, only two horses walked forward. Sellia had never formally met either of these men before, but she knew them both.

Though neither was mortal, Sellia could tell which of them had been human most recently. The one on the left looked at the world as if he were watching his old home burn to the ground. The One on the right watched the house burn as if His true love were still inside.

Moses shuddered, wagging its fins, suddenly free from its state of suspended animation, and resumed its hunt for Sellia.

The Fish Eater folded his arms beneath his garments. "Not the girl. Them," he nodded toward the riders, "Take as many of them with you as you can."

Moses seemed to obey, submerging its scaly hide beneath the sludge, creeping beneath the two horsemen trotting across the sea toward it. The horsemen watched the leviathan circle beneath them as the black water became translucent for them. Sellia watched the horses, wondering whether a horse spooked

121

while walking on water would drown or simply splash about. But the horses stood, as calm and as unwavering as their riders, one even swatting the flies off of its rear with its tail.

The monster emerged, its toothy grin showcasing the remains of its victims, each morsel a prize. Its mouth widened, set on devouring both with one dive.

The rider on the right touched the brim of Moses' nose. It stopped.

"It's OK," The Shining Man whispered in the creature's ear. "I'm here now." A crack formed where it was touched. It spread down its body and fins. The body split in two, breaking like bread across the ocean to feed the little fishes.

Sellia's reverence for the creature had been birthed from pure fear. Seeing it slain by The Shining Man gave her joy. She stood and began walking toward the approaching Horseman.

"Sellia! That's not the way you should go!" Bethesda clucked. With The Shining Man in sight, Bethesda was a poor mimic. The Shining Man stared into Bethesda's eyes. The ceramic christ crumbled to ash and wafted away on the back of a still wind.

The hairy and bulbous demons with their chattering smiles, draped with the shadows of Gehenna, fled back to hell's solace knowing that soon they would be in a place far worse.

But The Fish Eater, seemingly taking little notice of his vanishing entourage, focused more on Sellia as her wandering became a pursuit.

"Get back here!" The Fish Eater shouted, composure melting in the heat of the Son.

Sellia was at the end of the roof, but she kept walking after The Shining Man. Sellia's bare heel, cracked and sullied from the rocks, dirt, and glass, was cleansed by one step onto the purified ocean. She walked the pathway toward the riders, which was paved in crystal blue.

The Shining Man smiled at her. In His smile He knew her.

And Sellia began to recount who she was, all over again. The broad-banded steel rims of film reels slid into place on her mental projector as Sellia watched her story in an instant on the movie screen of her mind. The show was one she had seen before, and like most actresses, she hated watching herself. But with the promise of a better ending, she watched it again.

The first reel was the same. Before she had broken double digits in age, Sellia averaged one crumpled love note per month in elementary school, each one signed in illegible cursive by a Blake or a Paul. The Sellia of her teens had spent her evenings at frozen football games and school functions on dance floors covered with crepe paper. As the years progressed, she found the cinema to her liking. With each passing film—be it independent, classic, modern, or foreign—that graced the screen, she was there with beau in hand. She watched each, rarely taking a moment to blink. Every reel had been more fantastic than the last. She watched, ever aware that the fantasy in each film matched the degree of fantasy of her own life.

She knew niceties without the wisdom behind them. She knew style without Beauty. She knew love without ever knowing Love.

And now she knew why. The lights went up in the theater of her mind, and she saw nothing but The Shining Man's smile. In His smile of knowing, He did not see her past. Or her pain. Or that she was lonely. Or that she was dirty. Or that she was loved by twenty-three others she had gloated on. Or that anything in the passing world was particularly her fault.

The Shining Man saw something else. The lights turned down again and the film resumed. In those days before the double digits broke, Sellia would attend her slumber parties with her girlfriends. In those purposefully sleepless, giggling nights they would talk about their one true loves, even though they had never met them. As years passed, they would plan their imaginary weddings with "the one," the solitary name their future grooms commonly would become known under.

In her teens she composed poems and letters on her pillow. By reciting them as she stared out her window, she hoped that the one for her received them. She dreamed of him literally and in daily passing. She had a list of his qualities that she had kept close by her in high school. With each Saturday morning, Sellia would compare her Friday night date with her checklist. Her date always failed.

He was either too old, too young, too dumb, too smart, too smart-mouthed, too dependent on his mother, too dependent on his friends, talked too little, talked too much, liked her too much, liked her too little for her taste, or looked at too many other girls during the evening. One did not have a job, one did not have a car, one could not fit in with her family, and one was as picky as she.

But, I'm not picky, she thought.

The one was only supposed to be there for her. To laugh only when she did and when she needed it. The one had the right thing to say at the right time. The one knew where the itch was and scratched it just right. The one knew her hurt without ever having to be told of it. The one knew when to be quiet and knew the value of it. The one would never leave her when she needed him. The one would come and find her when she was hiding. He would find her even when she did not know she was lost.

By adulthood, she had given up her list and her search for the one, chalking him up as one of the myths parents tell their children, right alongside Santa Claus and "the goldfish is only sleeping."

But now, with only one look, she knew He was the One. As she watched each scene play out again, she could see The Shining Man had been there for each one. He walked by her on the football field in a muddy gold jersey. He sat on her bed at the slumber parties, His calloused hands with scars through the wrists extended in a game of cat's cradle.

"Hello, Sellia," The Shining Man said. The reel ended and spun 'round in the projector. The lights came up.

She was planning on saying something, shaking His hands, and playing ambassador to The Shining Man. But tears came instead, and she plodded across the water and leapt into His Carpenter's arms. He pulled her onto His regal white horse. She clung to Him, all of her wet tears turning dry as they dripped onto His shoulders.

At the same time as He was reunited with her, He was also with the rider on the left as they dismounted and approached

The Fish Eater on foot through the aquamarine pathway.

The Fish Eater stood. His regality still flowed as wine from a winepress. The Fish Eater drew his sword from its jewel-encrusted scabbard. It was four feet long, jagged, and black with blood as he unsheathed it. He looked to his Enemy, preparing to fight.

The Shining Man only spoke. A white-and-crimson handled sword jutted from His mouth with each pronouncement. The saints on horseback, the angels, Sellia, Sam, and Bob all heard Him speak, but no one could repeat what He was saying. They understood it, but without knowing how. *It was the most beautiful speech*, Sellia thought, *sweet yet horrible in meaning*. The words had been crafted in the millennia of oblivion before The Fish Eater, only to be honed in the millennia after the archangel's betrayal. It was delivered in tones of sorrow, disappointment, and anger.

When the masses looked back to The Fish Eater, he was on his knees, mortally wounded, his robes peeling off, his helmet cracking. His jewelry, carefully selected to be ornately terrifying, poured off of him like rain. He was naked.

Like a bird plucked of wings and feathers, he lay on the sanctuary roof. His eyes burned, puffy and red from the soot and sulfur of both of his worlds.

"Bob, come," The Shining Man said, looking to the rider on the left. "Put your foot on his head. Claim your victory."

To Sellia, Bob looked quite encumbered by the prospect of putting his heel on the tormentor. Bob walked across the uneven waterscape, stepping up to the roof of the chapel. Bob obeyed, his bare heel crushing the sullied head of the serpent.

The Shining Man looked around at His family. The angels were rejoicing, Bob and the rest of the saints were victorious, and Sellia was in Love. The Shining Man would have joined them in celebration, but He missed one.

He looked across the sea at Sam. Sam sat on his little island where he had been placed. And again time stopped. Angels ascending and descending were frozen, saints on horses halted, and the damned despot was immobilized, all trapped in one of time's chambers. All but Sam and The Shining Man.

The Shining Man walked across the glassy water toward Sam's island.

"Hello, Sam."

"Jesus," Sam said, "I—"

"Surprised to see Me?"

"No. And, yes."

The Shining Man smiled.

"I almost don't know what to say. We, well, we haven't spoken for so long," Sam said.

"We used to be close."

"Yeah, I know."

"I miss it."

"Really?"

"Yeah." The Shining Man sat down next to Sam on their little island of dirt. They stared out over the tableau before them, an apocalypse in still life.

"You make Me smile. I like it when you sing, too."

"Even though they're not praises?" Sam asked.

"Are you so sure they're not?" The Shining Man smiled again.

"I'm...I'm sorry. I didn't call out to You. I didn't come back. I didn't return. I got so fed up with everybody telling me what the rules were, I neglected Yours. I should've..."

Sam's repentance trailed off, but The Shining Man was quiet.

"Life was so hard. You start off knowing everything. You start off being the hero, and you end up an outcast. The past few days alone taught me that."

"Yeah, that's the way people are, aren't they?"

"Yeah, I guess You walked that road, too. I suppose You let me walk it so we'd have something in common." Sam picked up a stone and snapped it across the water.

"Not as cynical as that. I just want you to be like Me."

"Then let me just be like You. I'm human. I don't want the lesson; I want the quick fix!"

The Shining Man laughed. Not at him, but as when the son states the full extent of his knowledge, leaving the father knowing so much more. The Shining Man put His hand on Sam's shoulder and with His other hand skipped a stone across the ocean.

"Yeah, I know," Sam said.

"Are you ready to go?" The Shining Man asked.

"I can't go. I didn't call out to You like Sellia did. I didn't pick sides."

"Didn't you? She picked every side, and then she found me. You waited. But I can't force you to come. It's a choice." He smiled. "I'm in the boat, you're still in the tree, and I won't knock you out of it."

"Are you going to destroy the world?" Sam asked.

"Not yet. I'm going to redeem it first. Everything has a second chance." The Shining Man stood to leave, time clicking into place, resuming its silent countdown. The Shining Man spoke to the archangels, "Begin."

Sam took his eyes off The Shining Man and watched as the sky, not the clouds but the sky itself, punctured and poured celestial beings into the lesser world. Long-haired, inhuman, sexless creatures, each flapping six wings, swarmed from above. They were seven feet long, glowing and glorious, with long tails trailing fire and stardust after themselves. They appeared clean by human standards, but they seemed covered with something. They may have been drenched in gold dirt from heaven or the mud of myrrh from that celestial place, but there was no way for Sam or Sellia to know. The creatures came out of the single break in the sky and spread out from that fissure. With their tails they lit the firmament ablaze.

The gray sky turned to gold as it was lapped up by heavenly flame. Fire-dribbling clouds plummeted to the ocean. Sam arched his back and thrust his arm in the air in an apparent plea for shelter.

As fire rained around them, The Shining Man walked out upon the ocean away from Bob, Sellia, Sam, and The Fish Eater. Sam seemed to look out to sea after his Master. His eyes were fixed on The Shining Man.

And then The Shining Man began to glow brighter. White

light surfaced from His skin, shot out of His eyes, adorned His hair, emerged from His fingertips, and streamed from His mouth. He never lost His form, though He was glowing brighter than the sun.

The Shining Man had become so bright that Sellia, Bob, and half the saints looked away. But Sam looked on. He was the nearest and the only one still mortal. The scorching aura should have consumed him. But it never did.

The water level was dropping rapidly. Steam bled vertically from the water as the sea was seared by the Son. As the water level dropped around the throng, the seas churned and spun. As this caldron boiled it became a whirlpool. The steel buildings, unearthed by the receding tides, began melting, their molten innards pouring into the abyss. The Shining Man shone brighter as the dross from the earth was melted away and the flaws disappeared. The world would soon be a lump of clay that could be molded again.

"Wait!" Sam yelled from his perch. "I'm not afraid of eternity. I'm not afraid. Can't I be with you just a little longer?"

The Shining Man looked his way. *Come,* His eyes said.

Sam looked down at the violent abyss. Surely he must have misread, he thought, and looked again to The Shining Man.

Come!

Sam took one barefooted step forward onto the boiling ocean. The meat of his feet began melting away almost immediately. The pain was unbearable. Sam looked as though he would remove his foot.

There was not a hint of persuasion or affirmation from The Shining Man. The saints were silently cheering; Abraham, David, and Peter were rubbing their palms nervously. Sellia was wishing she could shout for him. But one thing they all noticed was that The Shining Man never took His eyes off of Sam.

Nor did Sam avert his gaze. He took another step. Streaming water sizzled beneath him like hot grease. Sam was in obvious agony. But in his agony a realization could be seen registering on his face; he was standing on the water.

Another step. Sam seemed to lean forward with every skin-peeling stride. It was apparent to all that he was still looking at The Shining Man.

Sellia thought for a moment as she watched. How hot was it? The Shining Man was burning brighter than she had ever glimpsed the sun, yet Sam was still able to walk. Even now, safe in His company, she could barely stand to gaze upon His brilliant countenance. *Sam should have been blind long before,* she thought. Surely, his frail body could never reach the perfect form of The Shining Man.

Sam had come halfway, his knees buckling with the heat. He still walked, each stride dedicated toward his destination, his gait and swagger now filled with purpose.

Though he made progress, Sam began to grow impatient. As fire ate him and torment threatened him to succumb, he was weary. At one point he tried to run, but he only tripped upon the blazing water.

The Shining Man winced and watched as Sam sunk a little and attempted to pull himself up. To Sellia it seemed that The Shining Man appeared to be struggling. He was wringing His hands, unable to watch or pick Sam up and carry him the rest of the way home.

The Shining Man puckered His lips and blew on Sam. A breeze of winter frost came welcomed onto Sam's face.

"That's cheating!" screamed The Fish Eater. "He shouldn't have help!"

Sam grew more confident and stood upright. The heat continued to burn the soles of his feet until they were nothing but giant blisters spewing water back into the burning lake. The heat grew more intense, but Sam stayed steady. The cool air continued to be poured out to him. Sam no longer showed pain. He was far beyond that point. His stride and gait convulsed a little with each step. His body was in shock.

Sam's eyes slowly closed sleepily as he grew faint. A broad smile resided confidently on his face. Sellia looked to The Shining Man. Sam was still only a little more than halfway across. Sam swayed for a moment, possibly having just come to this realization himself. He took another two steps before his body pitched forward, his legs still making the motions of moving. He fell into the arms of his Creator.

"Lord, I'm so sorry." Sam knelt in the fire, and he was cleansed before he had finished his sentence. The Shining Man picked him up as they wept.

"No more," The Shining Man cried. Sam found a niche in the cleft of His shoulders and allowed his own tears to collect there; and there they stayed. A horse of brilliant white splashed down into the ocean and pranced around Sam as the boy was reunited in his Father's embrace.

At this time, the archangels returned from their apparent world tour. Sellia looked up for a moment, though she still thought the light too intense, and saw as they began circling in the sky, weaving their threaded arcs around, seemingly without purpose.

They surrounded The Fish Eater. The fallen enemy lifted his scorned head to The Shining Man, and then to the sky as his fellow archangels swooped upon him like vultures. It took eight of them to seize him, as The Fish Eater fought them as a certain aquatic animal does on a hook that ensnares him. He wriggled and tried to kick his brothers until they each grabbed one of his limbs and carried him upward. But still he tried to break their grip.

Snap.

The Fish Eater leveraged the grip of the archangels, breaking his right arm. The sullied angel used this to his advantage, trying to squeeze his dislocated bones away from his onetime fellows, but they held on to his arm even harder, causing him to squeal in pain. Sellia had to cover her ears as The Fish Eater's scream of torment matched boB's earlier ones.

The Fish Eater continued his squirming, evermore angered. He sniped at each angel, calling each by name. And if one drew close, he bit them.

"I am your fair-haired golden child!" he screamed, "I spoke sanctity! I was clothed in it. I am more sanctimonious than you!" The Fish Eater craned his neck backward and saw the spinning cyclone of boiling water below him. Beyond the whirlpool was a vortex of black. Nothingness. Pure oblivion. The Pit. Like a hungry beast,

The Pit chewed on fire, air, and water, aching to devour him.

The Archangels looked back to The Shining Man. The Shining Man nodded. The Fish Eater was dropped and plummeted into the mouth of his torment.

As His family assembled and were seated on their horses, The Shining Man looked again up close at the world that He had created. He had made it good, then watched it become corrupted. He had vied for the affections of a fickle world in an on again-off again relationship that had defined the ages.

He turned His head to the earth itself and smiled again as He admired His own handiwork. His eyes peered across the globe, examining the nooks and crannies of the world that He had crafted against the grain. He took in the world, from the plains to the lonely mountaintop crags. He remembered when He first blew the dust off of them. He wanted to peel back the waters and look again at the rifts and the reefs up close. He wanted to show His work of art to His adopted and extended family of saints.

He would share the world with them before making it over again.

He seemed to know all along, before the inception of man, the Fall, the years of silence, the years of walking low among them, and the years of waiting, that He would be able to start all over again with His own true love.

As His true love looked on, The Shining Man cleared the pallet. In an instant He exploded; the light He had been permeating became tangible to the terrestrial world. The world dissipated in a blanket of white light that spread out among the unrestrained darkness.

The explosion ended, and Sellia watched as the light echoed in the expanse of the world, rebuilding and reclaiming all that she had known. The Grand Palisade Theatre, Narcissi Plaza, Charlatan Hotel, the Alamo Lounge, the sanctuary on the hill, Bob's house, West Erickson Bridge, and even Bethesda Pines Outlet Mall appeared—restructured, reset, and redeemed. Flames and smoke disappeared. The Pit was sealed, and the angry ocean calmed, sliding back into place. A word from the Creator healed the sky. Sellia looked up and saw that the soot-bearing clouds had been seared away and that the sky was blue again. But there was no sun. She opened her mouth to The Shining Man to complain, but in shock saw that He had replaced the sun, His countenance now shining in yellow just for her. Yellow ember and yellow rays lit the ocean from the shore to the depths and lit the land from skyscraper peaks to every hidden back alley. The Son forever would be with them.

The Shining Man then turned to the saints, among them Adam, Noah, Abraham, the real Moses, King David, Peter, Bob, the bum, Sellia, and Sam. They saw their world together.

And it was Good.

EPILOGUE

SELLIA AWOKE, NEVER KNOWING MONDAYS TO BE so beautiful. Yellow sunlight shone into her four walls of comfort that represented a completeness she had never known. Sellia lay in her bed, sleepy but not tired, and watched the precious embers of her color shimmer through the room.

The yellow sunlight spoke, "Good morning, Sellia." It was The Shining Man.

"Good morning," she smiled, warm, clean, and happy.

"I thought We'd go into town today."

Sellia yawned, covering her mouth with her pillow. Her eyes apologized needlessly. "You're not going to make me guess, right?"

"Maybe a little."

She flung the pillow at Him. He caught it. "We'll be busy with other things later today. Let's take some time off at first," The Shining Man said.

"Romantic outing? Picnic in the park. Ice skating. Tree climbing?"

"I thought We'd visit some old friends."

Sellia's lips burst into a grin as she giggled and leapt out of bed. She spun across her carpeted apartment and flung open her closet. There on a hanger lay her cotton dress, white and blameless, sashaying in her eyes. Removing it from its metal backbone, she dressed herself in the friendly garment and while grabbing her shoes dashed out her apartment door, which The Shining Man held open for her.

As They walked down the steps together arm in arm, Sellia neglected once again to count the number of steps on the fourteen/fifteen step staircase. As They reached the landing, Sellia looked up to Him to appreciate His features and the little things He did.

Their eyes met and they continued walking. They passed through the lobby, plush with furniture and tiled in marble. Golden columns marked the way to the bright glass door.

The doormen opened the door for The Couple as they exited the palatial townhouse. The doorman holding the left door smiled at them with perfect teeth through his trimmed beard, tilting his lopsided cap to greet them as they passed by. The Doorman to the right was The Shining Man. The Couple exited the mansion as the doormen waved good-bye.

Sellia and The Shining Man walked down the brilliant street. Perfect could only describe the surroundings as Sellia passed the refurbished familiar. Sellia noted that *perfect* did not mean visually clean, or grime-free. There was nothing sterile about this redeemed Earth. Dirt still lay on the ground; leaves on the sidewalks. But they were pure. It seemed to Sellia that all she had known before had been out of proportion. Color had been tweaked and filtered. Tastes, no matter how succulent, had been dull before. Touch, no matter how intimate, had only been awkward and hampered compared to what it was now.

Also perfect and seemingly at the centerpiece of the street, a blues club rose into the matching azure sky.

"I knew it," Sellia said. "I knew that's where We were going."

"Are you excited?"

"I can't wait!" she smiled at Him, placing her head on His shoulder.

The metal doors pushed open into a deep cerulean world. Rounded tables with long black skirts mushroomed from the hard wooden floor. Sellia slid with her shoes to the music across the open planks of the dance floor. Stamping her feet with rhythmic delight, she looked at the singer. Sam was on stage at the microphone, making up another song out of his imagination. The Shining Man was at the piano. They wore fedoras as they invented songs in perfect harmony:

When I was sad, you were sorrow,
When I was happy, you were glee,

Now that my heart can follow,
I follow you and I am free.

Sam smiled at Sellia. He twisted his lanky legs and twirled in place.

Sellia did the same.

Sam tapped his feet in rapid succession before jumping up and kicking the well-deserving air.

Sellia gave up and shrugged, smiling into the arms of The Shining Man as they danced into the blue. The piano stopped and the Two continued dancing without music.

"New song. Everybody, new song," Sam said, changing his beat. He looked to The Shining Man at the piano. "We ready?"

"We need one more to do this one," The Shining Man said. "David."

"David, son of Jesse, we're paging you for your much-needed services on the harpsichord," Sam said. David was relaxing in a booth with dark upholstery. "I know you'll be working under a handicap, but I think if you strum along you'll get the hang of it."

David got up and joined the band. Now a Trio, Sam looked out to the crowd.

"I see we got a lot of the old faces. Hey Bob! How's it goin'? No hard feelings."

Bob gave Sam a thumbs-up.

"This is for you regulars here tonight," Sam continued, "this afternoon, morning, whatever. One…ah-two…ah-thirty-three…"

Sam and The Shining Man were singing on stage together. But as they continued it became difficult for Sellia to figure out who was singing it to whom.

Bob sat in the corner with The Shining Man. "You're going to have to explain to me how blues music is still around when there's no weeping, crying, or sadness of any kind."

"Do I?" The Shining Man smiled behind His glass of wine.

Sellia drifted into The Shining Man's arms, closing her eyes in abiding contentment. She danced again. But she did not dance alone.

To Contact the Author

apocalypseofbob@yahoo.com